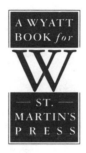

A WYATT BOOK *for*

W

— ST. —
MARTIN'S
PRESS

THE

PILTDOWN CONFESSION

— *A Novel* —

BY

IRWIN SCHWARTZ

A Wyatt Book for St. Martin's Press

NEW YORK

Design by Judith Stagnitto

Library of Congress Cataloging-in-Publication Data

Schwartz, Irwin.
    The Piltdown confession / Irwin Schwartz.
        p. cm.
    ISBN 0-312-11043-X
    1. Dawson, Charles, 1864–1916—Fiction.   2. Forgery of antiquities—England—History—Fiction.   3.   Archaeologists —England—Fiction.   4. Piltdown forgery—Fiction.   5. Forgers—England—Fiction.   I. Title.
    PS3569.C56575P54   1994
    813'.54—dc20   94-801
                                                            CIP

First edition: July 1994

10   9   8   7   6   5   4   3   2   1

ANNOTATOR'S FOREWORD

On a cold December day in 1908, in a village unknown outside the rural confines of Sussex in southern England, the first in a series of archeological discoveries destined to rock the foundation of science's understanding of human origins was made. The discoveries simultaneously threatened the Judeo-Christian Adam-and-Eve creation paradigm, which only fifty years earlier had been menaced by the publication of Charles Darwin's *On the Origin of Species*. The removal of a small number of bone fragments and artifacts from gravel pits near the obscure hamlet of Piltdown would foment a struggle for existence for both the religious and scientific communities. It would set priest against minister against pastor, and geologist against anatomist against anthropologist. It would ignite a war—of words and more—between men of the cloth and those of the spade. The thrusts and parries would last half a century, during which time the party or parties responsible for firing the first shot would remain unidentified.

It was not until 1953 that the fraudulent nature of Piltdown Man was finally confirmed. The cranial and mandibular remains were determined to have come from two quite different creatures. In addition to finding by fluorine dating that the two parts of the head were of different age, it was demonstrated that the cranium belonged to a relatively recent human being and the jaw was an orangutan's.

The identity of the perpetrators of the Piltdown hoax— a fraud which fooled some of the best scientists for almost half a century—remained unknown. Several very informed students of the incident have proposed candidates selected from a broad lineup of suspects. All of the accusatory evidence was circumstantial, however, and none could be made to stick. Until now.

We can at long last unambiguously and without equivocation specify the perpetrators of what turned out to be the grandest of illusions in the history of science. There were three co-conspirators, one of whom—the author of this memoir—died in 1916. At his request, the manuscript (which was written in the year he died) was to be maintained in safekeeping until 2008, the centennial anniversary of the clandestine deposit of a human parietal bone fragment. I obtained the original autograph (with the permission of the author's estate) and publish it now in its entirely, accompanied by annotations. The account weaves a tale threaded by intrigue and deception, scientific brilliance and Christian dogma, personal pride and professional passion, and murder.

PALEOLITHIC SKULL IS A MISSING LINK

Human Remains Found in England Similar in Some Details to Bones of Chimpanzee

FAR OLDER THAN CAVEMEN

Bones Probably Those of a Direct Ancestor of Modern Man, While Cavemen Died Out.

Special Cable to
THE NEW YORK TIMES.

LONDON, Dec. 18, 1912. — At a meeting of the Geological Society this evening the paleolithic human skull and mandible recently discovered on Piltdown Common, Sussex, formed the subject of papers by Charles Dawson, F.G.S., and Dr. Woodward, Keeper of the Geological Department of the British Museum, who was [sic] jointly responsible for the recovery and recasting of the skull, which was broken into fragments when it was unearthed by workmen.

Dr. Woodward said the skull proved to be very different from the skull of any class of man hitherto met with. It had the steep forehead of the modern man, with scarcely any brow ridges, and the only external appearance of antiquity was found in the occiput, which showed that in this early form the neck was shaped not like that of modern man but more like that of the ape. The brain capacity was only about two-thirds that of the ordinary modern man.

The mandible, Dr. Woodward added, differed remarkably from that of man. It agreed exactly with the mandible of a young chimpanzee. Still, it bore two molar teeth, which were human in shape. If these were removed it would be impossible to decide that the jaw was human at all. The skull differed so much from those of cavemen already found in Germany, Belgium, and France, that it was difficult at first sight to interpret it.

The new specimen, said Dr. Woodward, was proved by geological considerations to be very much older than the remains of these cavemen. It was interesting to note in this connection that the newly found skull was closely similar in shape to that of a very young chimpanzee, while the skull of the later cavemen had the brows of a full-grown chimpanzee. Therefore the changes which took place in the skull in successive races of early man were exactly similar to the changes which took place in the skull of the ape as it grew from youth to maturity.

Dr. Woodward said he was inclined, therefore, to the theory that the caveman was a degenerate offshoot of early man, and probably became extinct, while surviving modern man might have arisen directly from the primitive source of which the Piltdown skull provided the first discovered evidence.

Dr. Woodward, replying to a question as to the approximate date of the skull, told a reporter that it belonged to the Lower Pleistocene period, which could not be computed in terms of years. A dim conception of its antiquity could be gained from the fact that the gravel in which it was embedded must have been carried there by a stream which was now the Ouse, and which had since cut for itself a channel eighty feet deep and a mile distant from the spot. In the gravel, too, were relics of the elephant, mastodon, hippopotamus, and red deer, besides flint implements anterior to those used by the cave dwellers.

Charles Dawson

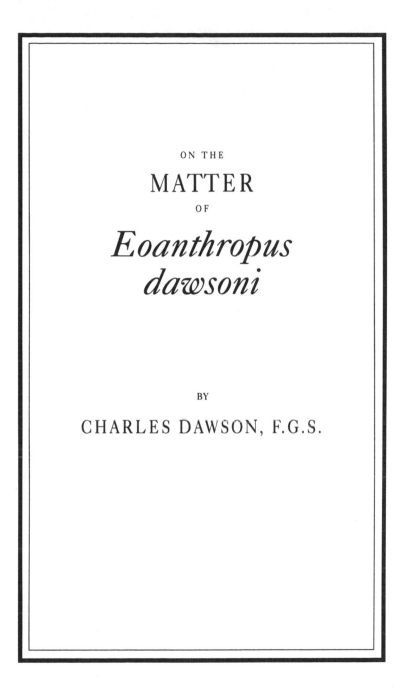

ON THE

MATTER

OF

Eoanthropus dawsoni

BY

CHARLES DAWSON, F.G.S.

This Chronicle, attested to by my hand
on this Seventeenth day of July in the
Year of Our Lord
One Thousand Nine Hundred and Sixteen, is
bona fide and authentic;

*SO SWORN IN THE GOOD AND GRACIOUS
NAMES OF HIS ROYAL MAJESTY AND
GOD ALMIGHTY!*

I was one of three co-perpetrators of the fraud which may be
referred to as the Piltdown hoax, or as the hoax of Sussex Man
("Eoanthropus dawsoni"). I uncategorically state—with incontestable and undeniable proof to follow—that it was I who surreptitiously deposited fabricated fossil remains and artifacts in
and around gravel-pits adjacent to the village of Piltdown, in the
County of Sussex, on 9 July 1908, in performance of the deception. I repeated the act of subterfuge several times at the initial
site, and at one other site, until 1915. I maintained anonymity at
the time, and determined to remain mute until my death. This
conduct was elicited by an unremitting fear of assassination.

I have been blessed with the good fortune of having made the discovery of three legitimate new species for which the signal honour was having my surname appended to their genera.[1] I am also, however, accursed with the stigma of having my name attached to a fabricated species. It is *Eoanthropus* (variously, *Eocanthropus*) *dawsoni* that will no doubt forever impugn my credentials for intellectual honesty. At the outset of this reminiscence I feel obligated to plead that, for such a corruption of personal and professional integrity, I am truly repentant; for I participated in perverting the science I love so much.

My 1913 report on the discovery of Sussex Man read, in part:

---

[1] *Iguanodon dawsoni*, a dinosaur; *Plagiaulax dawsoni*, a mammal; *Salaginella dawsoni*, a plant.

Several years ago I was walking along a farm road close to Piltdown Common, Fletching (Sussex), when I noticed that the road had been mended with some peculiar brown flints, not usual in the district. On inquiry, I was astonished to learn that they were dug from a gravel bed on the farm, and shortly afterwards I visited the place, where two labourers were at work digging the gravel for small repairs to the roads. As this excavation was situated four miles north of the limit where the occurrence of flints overlying the Wealden strata is recorded, I was much interested and made a close examination of the bed. I asked the workmen if they had found bones or other fossils there. As they did not appear to have noticed anything of the sort, I urged them to preserve anything that they might find. Upon one of my subsequent visits to the pit, one of the men handed to me a small portion of an unusually thick human parietal bone. I immediately made a search, but could find nothing more; nor had the men noticed anything else. The bed is full of tabular pieces of iron-stone closely resembling this piece of skull in colour and thickness; and although I made many subsequent searches, I could not hear of any further find nor discover anything—in fact, the bed seemed quite unfossiliferous. It was not until some years later, in the autumn of 1911, on a visit to the spot, that I picked up, among the rain-washed spoil-heaps of the gravel-pit, another and larger piece. . . .[2]

This report was completely false.

I was born the son of Hugh Dawson, a barrister, at

---

[2] The quote is from Dawson and Arthur Smith Woodward's paper, "On the Discovery of a Palæolithic Human Skull and Mandible in Flint-bearing Gravel Overlying the Wealden (Hastings Beds) at Piltdown, Fletching (Sussex)," published in 1913 in the *Quarterly Journal of the Geological Society* 69, pp. 117–144.

Fulkeith Hall, Lancashire, on 11 July 1864. Taking the example of my father, I entered the legal profession as a solicitor, but even as a schoolboy at the Royal Academy, Gosport, my schoolmaster, S. H. Beckles—himself a geologist—had nourished my interest in scientific pursuits. I practised law in Hastings throughout that decade, then moved to Lewes, with chambers in Uckfield nearby.[3] By the turn of the century I had established a successful and lucrative business. My activities comprised the stewardship of several local manorial estates, including the Barkham farm, about which more later. In addition, I served as clerk to the local urban council and to a variety of magistrates.

My interest in natural history had begun at a rather early age and, by 1885, I had collected a large variety of fossil specimens from the Wealden formations surrounding Hastings. The most significant of these were handed over to the British Museum. Among that assemblage, I am happy to say, is a rather fine example of *Lepidotus mantelli*, a local ganoid fish.[4] Perhaps because of my youthful energy (which, in retrospect, seems inexhaustible), I was awarded the title of Honorary Collector by the Museum.[5] I continued exploring within and

---

[3] Dawson remained at Lewes until his death on August 10, 1916, due to a sequence of pyorrhea alveolaris, anemia and, finally, septicemia.

[4] A ganoid scale is a primitive structure having several layers of enamel-like material (ganoin) on the upper surface and laminated bone below.

[5] The Hastings Museum now houses Dawson's private collection. It contains, among other artifacts, a "Toad in the Hole" (a piece of flint bearing a fossilized toad), flint implements, bone fragments, antique glass, a medieval anvil.

collecting from the Weald, having presently been joined by two students who were attending the Jesuit College in Hastings, Félix Pelletier and Marie-Joseph Pierre Teilhard de Chardin. Teilhard was, I remember thinking, particularly intelligent and perceptive.[6] This triumvirate of tireless explorers was fortunate to have found the remains of a second new mammal, *Diprioden valensis*, from an area that was revealing itself as a treasure-trove containing vast paleontological riches. We would celebrate our successes and bemoan our failures (it mattered not which) over more than a few pints at the local pub, The Lamb, where we would often muse over "Ice-Age Man".

My collateral interest in geology likewise proved rewarding; I discovered at Heathfield a cache of natural gas and reported this to the Geological Society of London in 1898.[7] In addition, the Weald surrendered to me a deposit of zinc blende.[8] So captivated by the natural sciences was I that I neglected somewhat my profession as solicitor, albeit with not too much concern since I was rather financially comfortable.

And so, I was quite an active non-professional partici-

---

[6]Teilhard was a theology and vertebrate paleontology student at Ore Place in Hastings between 1908 and 1912. It was during this interval that he read the evolutionary philosophy of Henri Bergson in *L'Evolution créatrice* (1907). This work was to represent a significant influence on the development of Teilhard's radical *Weltanschauung*. He was ordained on August 24, 1911.

[7]Dawson was elected a Fellow of the Geological Society (F.G.S.) in 1885 at the age of twenty-one.

[8]A sulfide used as a fuel.

pant among the scientific community (the *bona fide* professionals referred to me as an "amateur", and with no small
measure of disdain). My hard-worked-for discoveries were
invariably accepted for study and storage by the Geological Society and the Museum, respectively, but my tracts
and analyses were rarely, if ever, received with the distinc-
tion afforded to members of the inner circle.[9] Had I
not loved the excitement of paleo-archaeology and paleoanthropology as much as I did, I would surely not have
felt so strongly the overt and implied stings from gentlemen whom I considered colleagues sharing in the discovery of the key that unlocks the mysteries of human
descent. However, since my interest in finding new information concerning whence *Homo* came and how he came
to be the way he is bordered on intellectual obsession, I
refused to permit the "established" scientific community—Smith Woodward among them[10]—the courtesy or
the satisfaction of passing what I considered poor judgement on my interpretive competence, and certainly not
on my investigative abilities. There is indeed a sea of

---

[9]To be sure, when papers concerning the Piltdown finds were presented to
the Geological Society, Dawson would present issues related to the geology
of the site and Arthur Smith Woodward (see note 10) would read his
interpretations of the bones and artifacts. It was Smith Woodward who
controlled the "meat" of the presentation, although it was Dawson who had
"found" the original relics.

[10]Arthur Smith Woodward (1864–1944) was a vertebrate paleontologist by
trade. He was also Keeper of Geology at the British Museum (Natural
History) from 1901 to 1924. It was he who first reconstructed and interpreted
the human remains found at Piltdown. Woodward was knighted in 1924.

difference between one's being intelligent and one's being educated. I would not let stand the scientific community's *sotto voce* insults to me, and by extension, to other *amateurs-en-armes*. I would soon become resolute to demonstrate to that haughty aggregate that there was not necessarily much correspondence between being a Doctor of Philosophy and doing good work in science. I was, in short, disposed—as the recently-popular Sigmund Freud would put it—to deflate more than several egos. Indeed, even as early as 1901 I had begun to consider serving up just desserts in recompense for the arrogance of the scientific community.

Activity concerning the origins of *Homo sapiens* had become quite brisk following the discovery of the Java Man and the Heidelberg jaw.[11] It had, in fact, become quite clear more than a century ago that human beings

---

[11] The so-called Heidelberg jaw was found in the Mauer Sands of Germany in 1907. The jaw, which is unusually large and thick (and virtually chinless), became the second "new" type of human to be found within the span of a decade (Java Man [1891] was the other). It was characterized and christened *Homo heidelbergensis* by Otto Schoentensack, but is today considered to be of *Homo erectus* stock. The mandible dates from about 400,000 years ago, making it contemporaneous with *erectus* remains recovered in China.

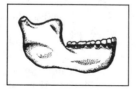

The Heidelberg jaw (William Howells, *Mankind So Far* [Garden City, NY: Doubleday & Co., 1946])

had existed during the remote past. Implements and other artifacts associated with ancient human activity had been recovered *in situ* among the remains of extinct fauna. Such discoveries compelled a re-evaluation of how long sapiens had in fact been walking the Earth.

The discovery of the Neanderthal[12] remains not only made it clear that humans had existed deeper in time than was previously thought but—equally and perhaps more significantly—had not always existed in their present form.

At about the time of the passing of Her Majesty Queen Victoria, in 1901, the secular and the devout were in turmoil over the incontestable brilliance and assumed heresy of Darwin's *Origin*.

In 1908 there were but three physical specimens that attested to the previous existence of human beings in a form somewhat different from those alive today. There were the Neanderthal remains found in 1857, the Java Man found in 1891, and the Heidelberg jaw which was

---

[12] The Neanderthals (*Homo sapiens neandertalensis*) are currently considered to be either an evolutionary dead end that was genetically absorbed by modern humans (*Homo sapiens sapiens*), or ancestors of modern humans lying in a direct line of descent. In either case, they survived until as recently as 30,000 years ago.

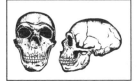

The skull of the *La Chapelle-aux-Saints* Neanderthal Man (After Howells, 1946)

unearthed in 1907. These discoveries precipitated vociferous debate as to whether or not Man had evolved from some ape-like precursor. More evidence—data in the form of the remains of ape-to-Man linkages—would be required, however, before the majority of the scientific community would consider accepting proof of Darwin's theory of human descent. There was already a large faction comprising students of geology and anthropology who had been given to the theory of evolution based only on what they perceived as its incontrovertible logic. However, pure logic was not physical evidence, and sceptics wanted to see more proto-human remains. Unfortunately, ancient hominid remains are not very common; nor are they easy to find.[13] These three circumstances—the excitement aroused by Darwin's theory, the suspicion, but lack of proof, that Man had evolved from ape-like ancestors, and the dearth of available physical evidence— would be the foundation for my scheme of retribution, as well as the source of sufficient protection against immediate detection and exposure. I would provide the evidence (which would be well-received in reversal of the current absence of an ancestral Englishman), stir the stew-pot of

---

[13] This paucity of fossil finds still exists, due perhaps, as some paleontologists suggest, to the rarity of early *Homo*. Indeed, by today's standards, australopithecines and archaic humans could well have been classified as endangered species.

debate, and play the rôle of innocent, yet active, participant. My first two assignments, then, were to fabricate an appropriate ancestor and to find a suitable locus of deposit for his bones and personal effects. The latter task was much easier to accomplish than the former, for I already had the perfect site in mind. By early 1908 I was ready to act.

I met my first co-conspirator, Pierre Teilhard de Chardin, in 1909. He was then attending the Jesuit College in Hastings where, in addition to his theological studies, he sated his keen interest in geology and paleontology. Indeed, he became quite competent in those disciplines for which the groundwork, he told me, had been laid while he was in Egypt for a three-year stay. Teilhard, who was ordained a Roman Catholic priest in 1911, had a certain academic inquisitiveness and—more significantly—an intellectual intensity and independence which I found refreshing and stimulating. It had become obvious from the beginning that we enjoyed each other's companionship, sharing in both esoterica and, I must admit, occasional blue humour. The esoterica grew more arcane and the humour more blue as the quantity of ale consumed increased and the hour advanced. Teilhard was to become a good and trusted friend. And that friendship, I knew, would last a lifetime. Although he was but twenty-eight years old (seventeen years my junior) when we first made acquaintance, I immediately perceived a depth of discriminating sophistication that belied his yet-tender years.

But beneath the *camaraderie* and entertaining humour of Teilhard resided a deeper and darker personage. He confided to me that he had avowed service to an institution with which he was rather at odds. He was moreover upset by the recently-consummated alliance between the newly-established Protestant Evangelical faction in England and its analogue in the United States. I would spend many hours at the The Lamb listening to him bemoan the Roman Church's intractably dogmatic theology and the conservative Evangelical threat both to his Church and to society at large. There dwelt under the outwardly gay spirit of Teilhard a very burdened young man. His most immediate philosophical difficulty, he told me, was reconciliation of the incongruity between his allegiance to Christianity and his devotion to Evolution—a very difficult task indeed.

The remaining co-conspirator was a years'-long friend, Sir Arthur Conan Doyle, creator of the fictional private detective Sherlock Holmes.

Doyle resides in Crowborough, a town situated not too far north of Uckfield. He has a curious, but well-balanced, mixture of interests including, of late, an engrossment with spirituality. He is also kept quite busy over social issues and, in that connexion, has taken up such activities as being President of the Divorce Reform Association, which supports incompatibility alone as sufficient grounds for marital annulment. Doyle is involved too in improving the teaching of deaf-and-dumb persons, and has for many years advocated the construction of a Channel tunnel so that travel between England and the Continent could be more easily accomplished. In addition, he curiously supports a ban on the use of feathers in women's hats and clothing, a position I consider to verge on the eccentric.

However, it is Doyle's amateur sleuthing—his insatiable interest in criminology (as evidenced by his active participation in the investigation of the "Jack the Ripper" murders during the '80's and '90's)—that has the greatest bearing on the adventure I am about to describe.

The East Sussex countryside was, as always, lovely—particularly so on this beautiful second day of June, 1912. I harboured a certain pride in being accompanied by a Continental friend; I could unabashedly bask in what some may have nominated as Island conceit. As the three of us were being transported to the farm by motor (Dr Arthur Smith Woodward was also present), I could not help but notice the interest with which Teilhard surveyed the terrain. He was clearly engrossed in making sense of this hill, that dale, and the long-term geological influence of the River Ouse on the area in general. He was quite rapt in thought, endeavouring to understand the significance of what I had previously described to him as being at once beautiful and bountiful. At last I broke the contented silence of our cab ride from Uckfield Station to Barkham Manor[14] in Piltdown.

"We have arrived, gentlemen. Set your baggage at the edge of the road and let us proceed immediately to the site."[15] I paid the driver and we began walking the few hundred yards to the Piltdown gravel-pit.

---

[14] The evidence suggests that this meeting took place on June 2, 1912, based on a letter from Teilhard to his parents dated the 3rd.

[15] In the same letter of June 3, 1912, to his parents, Teilhard wrote: "We embarked in a motor-car, with the elements of a picnic, which took us three miles, mostly across Uckfield Park, and deposited us at the place where the hunt was on. This was a stretch of grass 4 or 5 metres in width, beside a wooded glade leading to a farm. Under this grass there is a layer of pebbles, about 50 centimeters thick, which they are digging up, bit by bit, for road mending. A man was there to shift the earth for us. Armed with spades and sieves, etc., we worked for hours and eventually with success." The Piltdown site's relation to Barkham Manor is shown below.

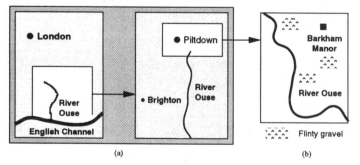

(a)   (b)

The Piltdown site: (a) general map showing part of south-east counties of Kent and Sussex, with the inset showing the general location of Piltdown; (b) a more detailed geographical map of the district surrounding Barkham Manor.

Our visit did not go unnoticed.[16]

On 20 June 1912, Teilhard and I met at The Lamb over supper and ale. We began the evening quietly enough by almost telepathically commencing the conversation with the same topic. It had been only two months before, on 14th April, that the tragedy of the liner *Titanic* had occurred. The subject pervaded Everyman's thoughts, having shocked the world at large and, in particular, the Commonwealth. Of the 2,201 passengers and crew aboard, only 712 survived. How could such a travesty have occurred? we asked. Wasn't the modern scientific community sophisticated enough to prevent the planet's leading ocean-going nation from sponsoring such carnage? Was my native Britain to be forever humiliated by a ship's captain who could not vouch for the safety of his passengers and crew? Were there really different treatments afforded first- and second-class passengers? Teilhard and I were appalled both by the failure of

---

[16] As Smith Woodward pointed out in his book, *The Earliest Englishman* (London: Watts, 1948), "[A]nd on the following Monday morning the local constable appeared at Mr Dawson's office in Uckfield (where he was Clerk to the Magistrates), stating that he had a report to make. Mr. Dawson, as usual in such cases, admitted the constable, and was surprised to learn from him that 'three toffs [persons of superior social status], two of them from London, had been digging like mad in the gravel at Barkham, and nobody could make out what they were up to.' Mr. Dawson's embarrassment may be imagined, but he remained calm and quietly explained to the constable that there were flints in the neighborhood, and perhaps the men he reported were merely harmless seekers of these flints. He then showed some of the flints to the constable, explained their interest, and asked him to look out and report on any that he might find in certain parts of his beat."

This is a photograph of Arthur Smith Woodward (on the right) and myself. Smith Woodward is sifting through soil in search of bones and artifacts. I do not know the name of the lad standing in the background. He happened to come by and watched us for several minutes, then left soon after the photo was snapped.

navigational science to accomplish such a simple task as crossing the Atlantic and by the unforgivable trespass of not providing adequate life-saving equipment. We were, I must say, as angry as we were aggrieved. I told Teilhard—and I knew he would take it in the correct light— that the Bishop of Winchester, upon learning of the disaster, had self-servingly appealed: "When has such a mighty lesson against our confidence and trust in power, machinery and money been shot through the nation? The *Titanic*, name and thing, will stand for a monument and warning to human presumption." Teilhard grinned and nodded his assent, as if to say that it was indeed Man who was responsible for the debacle, not God.

The evening at the pub proceeded splendidly. Both Teilhard and I finished an adequate supper of sausages and cabbage (I drew a hearty laugh from him when I told him tongue-in-cheek that this would represent the best British cuisine he could expect). Presently our table was approached by a beaming man.

"Ah, Pierre", I said, "I should like you to meet my good friend, Freddie 'The Barn' Handart. His size betrays the source of his nickname, doesn't it? Freddie's the piano-player here, and he knows every piece of music ever written. Buy him a pint, and he'll sing and play any song you like. Buy *me* another, and I'll sing along with him."

I then betrayed my heretofore well-protected secret of not being able to consume very much. "By my count, I've already put down four pints", I said with mock intellectuality. "I know this, Pierre, after having given careful mathematical consideration to the eight empty glasses in front of us, and the half as many spent jiggers in front of you. Clever, eh?" I suddenly realised that, somewhat out of character, I had become a bit tipsy. No matter; I was amongst friends.

"Freddie! *La Marseillaise*. Play the *Marseillaise* for *mon ami français. Pierre, écoutez, s'il vous plaît.*"

"Allons, enfants de la patrie,
Le jour de gloire est arrivée . . ."

Before the end of the first verse, the whole pub was singing along with us in butchered French, albeit with pitched enthusiasm. Teilhard, wearing civilian clothes, was never suspected of being a man of the cloth. To my good friends at The Lamb, he was merely another good friend—a Frenchie, they quickly recognised, but one who enjoyed the basic entertainments of ale and conviviality, as well as one who sincerely enjoyed the company of proud, hard-working rural men. In point of this fact, Teilhard graced our ears with a French ditty which, I remember, was called *"Mademoiselle d'Armentières"* (and which was appreciated by the crowd not for its lyrics, of course, but for its performer's animated mime). I strained to the limit my almost-non-existent recollection of schoolboy French to appreciate the subtlety of the words until I realised they were not subtle at all. I could now clearly see the source of the respect and admiration given Teilhard by others. He was simply an affectionate, fun-loving fellow who had the ability to secure the friendship of twenty people at a time. I was proud to be counted among them.

Freddie finished his entertainment for the evening to a

rousing round of applause, Teilhard gracefully tipping
the piano-player a shilling. Finally, Freddie played and
we all sang a solemn rendition of "God Save the King."
Teilhard, to the surprise and unabashed satisfaction of the
crowd, sang along fluently. The sounds of revelry had by
then subsided and the pub emptied out. The workmen
returned to their families for rest in anticipation of the
next hard day's labour. I ordered a round of brandies. The
proprietor—an old acquaintance—brought two snifters,
left the bottle on the table, and went home for the night.
Teilhard and I were alone.

I poured our drinks and we toasted our friendship.
Then I said, "Pierre, I should like to speak seriously to
you. Now that we are alone, I want to tell you something
which will make you and one other man the only persons
other than I who possess this knowledge. I am going to
entrust you with certain information. This is not, however, a confession of the type to which you are accus-
tomed, Father. This is one friend speaking to and sharing
with another. Feel however you may wish personally
about what I tell you, Pierre, but I implore you to hold
what I am going to say between us."

Our mood had suddenly shifted from one of gay cele-
bration to earnest sobriety. Teilhard looked me directly
in the eyes and, without his saying so much as a syllable,
I knew that my secret would be safe with him.

Although the clock had just struck midnight, and I
mentioned that my soliloquy might consume rather a

large amount of time, Teilhard warmly assured me that he was intent on listening to what I had to tell him.

I refreshed our snifters and began.

I commenced by explaining to Teilhard my move to Uckfield in 1890, where I established my practice as a solicitor. It was during the following year that I sent to Dr Arthur Smith Woodward a tooth he was later to describe as having belonged to a heretofore unknown species of *Plagiaulax*, a Cretaceous[17] Wealden mammal. I continued to dig in and around the Wealden area assiduously during my studies of Hastings Castle, several Lavant caves, a Roman encampment at Pevensey, and a skeletal excavation near Eastbourne. In 1899, I believe it was, I made the discovery of a gravel-bed at Piltdown Common, not too far from Barkham Manor, at which I was employed as steward at the time. I was indeed astonished to find such a deposit since it contained peculiar brown flints which to my knowledge had never been seen so far to the north. Given the general nature of the contents of the gravel-pit, I thought it might possibly hold fossiliferous remains, and accordingly asked the workmen to be on the look-out for any bones or fossils they might uncover during their labours. It was not until 1908 that two workmen presented me with fragments of what they

---

[17] A geological period dating to more than 150 million years ago.

thought resembled a fragmented coconut. One of them had shattered the whole with his pickaxe, and gave me a small piece, which happened to be a human left parietal bone.

"It was in fact *I* who had placed an almost-complete human calvaria[18] in the pit the night before", I confessed. "I feigned almost uncontrollable excitement and tipped the workman liberally for his recovery of the skull fragment. It was at this precise point, Pierre, that my hoax was inaugurated. I had conceded my first lie. To bolster the credibility of the 'find', as well as to reinforce my confidence in the success of the perfidious act, I contacted Samuel Woodhead.[19] At my invitation, he joined me in continuing the search for other fragments, but we were, to my disappointment, quite unsuccessful in that endeavour. My fear was that the remaining fragments had disappeared along with the gravel that had been removed for road-paving.

"I still paid occasional visits to the pit, but it was not until several years later that, when having a look over the rain-washed spoil-heaps, I lighted on a larger piece of the same surreptitiously deposited skull which included a portion of the left supra-orbital border.[20] At about the

---

[18] The skullcap, or top of the head.
[19] Samuel Allinson Woodhead (1862–1943), a chemistry instructor at Uckfield Agricultural College and a close friend of Dawson's.
[20] The bony ridge above the eyebrows. A prominent supra-orbital ridge is what gave the Neanderthals their "beetle-browed" appearance.

same time, in August of 1911, I 'found' a hippopotamus tooth fragment. On 14 February 1912, I crossed the Rubicon by writing to Smith Woodward:

> I have come across a very old Pleistocene bed overlying the Hastings Bed between Uckfield and Crowborough which I think is going to be interesting. It has a lot of iron-stained flints in it, so I suppose it is the oldest known flint gravel in the Weald.
>
> It contained a portion of a human (?) skull which will rival *H. Heidelbergensis* in solidity.

"First unable to come at my invitation because of bad weather and a rail strike, and then indisposed to make the trip to Sussex because of a previous commitment in Berlin to examine Cretaceous dinosaur remains recently discovered in East Africa, Smith Woodward was at last free to examine the Piltdown site on Saturday, 2 June 1912."

I then reminded Teilhard that I had prepared for him at my home that same Saturday morning a hearty English breakfast, and readied a picnic lunch (which featured French wine in honour of our friendship) in anticipation of Smith Woodward's arrival.

"You will remember this occurrence clearly since it was only eighteen days ago that our threesome took the train from Lewes to Uckfield, drove to Barkham Manor, and then walked along the path to the gravel-pit", I told Teilhard. "It was on that day that you found the flint eolith[21] and the *Stegodon* molar,[22] both of which I planted in the pit. It was at that point, too, my friend, that you were unwittingly drawn into my web of deception."

I waited for a reaction from Teilhard as I poured him another brandy, and he responded with an almost imperceptible curl of a grin.

"Continue, please", was all he said.

"You may also remember Smith Woodward's reaction to your finding the elephant molar that day. He was like a child with a new toy.[23] He, too, was deceived. But unlike you, Pierre, Smith Woodward will never know the truth, for it is he who will become my principal vehicle for humiliating the scientific community."

Another smile from Teilhard; this time, wider—much wider.

We finally left the pub at about half past one in the morning. We were both tired and somewhat overwhelmed

---

[21] The famous stone tool, designated E606 by the British Museum, is being referred to here. It was considered to have been a very fine specimen of well-worked flint. *Eolith* means "dawn stone." The Eolithic is the old Stone Age.

[22] *Stegodon* is a genus of primitive Asiatic Pliocene and Pleistocene mammals that have molar teeth with relatively broad enamel ridges and little cement, and thus are intermediate between elephants and mastodons.

[23] Teilhard's June 3, 1912, letter contains a gold mine of tidbits. About his discovery of the elephant molar, Teilhard wrote that "I myself laid hands on the fragment of an elephant's molar. This find considerably enhanced my reputation with Woodward, who jumped on the piece with the enthusiasm of a youth, and all the fire that his apparent coldness covered came out. . . . This first tooth of an elephant impressed me in the way another man is impressed by bringing down his first snipe."

by the merry-making as well as the victuals and intellectual fare of the evening. This led to the decision for
Teilhard to stay the night at my home. I knew that my
wife, Hélène,[24] would not object since she and Teilhard
got along famously, in large measure due to her having
been born in France. Teilhard and I also agreed that we
would meet two evenings hence, this time in a more
sedate setting.

We chose to ride by carriage to Crowborough from my
home in Lewes and dine at one of the better establish-
ments there. The restaurant I selected was a rather well
appointed one with private booths decorated in the best
of Victorian fashion. Fine woods, elegant brass accoutre-
ments, and soft leather seats gave it a warm personality.
The tables boasted the finest linen and featured tastefully
chosen cutlery and silver plate. Hanging on the walls were
several quite beautiful Wedgwood designs, purchased at
the Potteries in Staffordshire. The lighting produced a
rich golden cast and was most relaxing. Hidden behind
a red velvet curtain, a string quartet whispered chamber
music. This being a Friday evening, the gentlemen were
dressed with moderate formality, and the ladies were

---

[24] *Née* Hélène Postlethwaite (1859–1917) in Bordeaux of Irish stock. A
widow, she married Dawson in 1905. She had a son and a daughter by her
first husband.

wearing fine cotton and silk dresses. Teilhard wore his dog-collar.

My plan was to expound on my narrative of the first evening (the specific purpose being to relate how and where I had obtained the bones and artifacts, and how I prepared them for deposit), but Teilhard expropriated my blueprint for the evening with words that took me completely by surprise: "I should like to hear more details of your Piltdown activities, but to-night, Brother Charles, *I* have somewhat of a confession to make to you", he said. I encouraged him to speak his fill.

"Since a man's present rests upon the foundation of his past", he began, "perhaps it would serve us well, Charles, if you knew some details of my early life. It isn't very often that a priest can take into his confidence a non-cleric with that level of trust usually reserved for another man of the cloth. My faith in you is that much greater, my friend, since you are not bound to secrecy by ecclesiastical edict, but will hold to yourself what I have to say only as a function of fraternity and honour."

Teilhard insisted we have an *apéritif* before dinner. I accepted his suggestion and urged him to commence.

"As you know, Charles", he began, "it seems that from virtually the moment of my birth[25] I have had an insatiable

---

[25] May 1, 1881, at Sarcenat.

interest in natural history. In fact, my earliest memory—
my very first!—taught me about the non-fixity of nature.
My mother[26] had snipped off a few of my curls. I picked
one up and held it close to the fire. The hair was burnt
up in a fraction of a second. A terrible grief assailed me; I
had learnt that I was perishable. What used to grieve me
as a child was the insecurity of things. I used to treasure a
plough-hitch I had taken as my own, believing myself rich
with a wealth incorruptible, everlasting. And then it turned
out that what I possessed was just a bit of iron that had
rusted. At this discovery I threw myself on the lawn and
shed the bitterest tears of my existence! Despite what seemed
to me at the time an emotional agony, my father[27] encouraged my continued enthusiasm for natural history.

"In 1892 I entered the Jesuit school of Nôtre-Dame de
Mongré in Villefranche-sur-Saône. It was during my years
at the school[28] that I realised that I would dedicate my
life in devotion to Christ. It seemed to me as though God
offered me this vocation to leave the world. You can well

---

[26] Berthe-Adèle de Dompierre d'Hornoy, a great-grand-niece of Voltaire,
who married Emmanuel Teilhard de Chardin in 1875.

[27] Alexander Victor Emmanuel Teilhard de Chardin (1844–1932). He is
described warmly by his niece, Marguerite Teillard-Chambon: "A humanist
with a strong cultural bent, he was a wide reader, particularly in history; he
was a sound director of his children's reading, too, superintending their
Latin lessons himself until they were ready for secondary school. Another of
his contributions to the formation of their minds was to inculcate in them
an interest in natural objects, and to encourage them to make natural history
collections: birds, stones."

[28] 1892–1897.

imagine that once I was certain that I was not mistaken, I answered the call. All that I needed was for our Lord to make me feel unmistakably what He wanted of me and to give me the generosity of spirit that was required.

"In 1899 I entered my novitiate in Aix, and on 25 March 1901, I took my first vows at Laval to become a Jesuit. It was in that same year that the Jesuits withdrew to the Channel Islands due to legislation in France directed against religious orders. The years of my juniorate[29] were thus spent at Bon-Secours on the island of Jersey. The period on Jersey was punctuated by familial tragedy. In 1902 my eldest brother, Albéric, passed on at Sarcenat and my younger sister, Marguerite-Marie, became seriously ill with pleurisy. In 1904 my sister Louise died at the age of twelve of meningitis. I was relieved to have completed my juniorate in 1905, at which time I was assigned to teach chemistry and physics at the Jesuit College of the Holy Family in Cairo. And, as you know, Charles, last year the Lord took my dear sister Françoise.[30]

---

[29] 1902–1905.

[30] She succumbed to smallpox at the age of thirty-two in Shanghai, where she had been superior of the old people's home sponsored by the Little Sisters of the Poor. Her religious name was Sister Marie-Albéric du Sacré Coeur. Upon her death, Teilhard wrote to his parents (June 7, 1911): "How many times has she not spoken to me of her desire to go to God and to see Him as soon as possible. . . . Our Lord is rewarding her before her time; and we have not even the right to regret the good she would have done if she had lived longer. It is a beautiful life which fulfils the designs of God. In Françoise you have found and given to God a saint; you could not dream of a finer future for your child."

Thus, by the time of my ordination[31] I had become hard-
ened to the tragedy of losing loved ones. My greatest
childhood fears concerning the mortality of flesh and the
impermanance of substance had come true.

"My earliest years, then, were bridled by what I thought
were legitimate questions, the Church's answers to which
seemed unassailably contradictory and unfathomable. Was
the goodness of God manifest by His premature taking of
a large group of my family? Could God's creations and His
creative methodology be subject to scientific inquiry? Was
not Darwinian evolution the mechanism responsible for the
vast variety of life on the Earth, and for its extinction? Is
mankind the pinnacle of evolutionary biology? If answered
in the affirmative, can Man *further* progress physically and
spiritually to an end-point—an Omega point, if you will—
of perfection? Was I truly a sinner at birth as a function of
Original Sin? Can Man never divest himself of that sinful
birthright? Will humankind evolve to the Omega point to
find itself one with Christ, or is oneness with Him an
unreachable goal? Are Body and Soul truly inseparable?
Can not groups of persons, rather than only individuals,
be blessed and enjoy salvation? Questions, and more questions. I have all my life been a fount of questions, and
now I find myself part of an institution that harbours
neither tolerance for nor understanding of questioners.

---

[31]Teilhard was ordained by Monsignor Amigo, Bishop of Southwark, on
August 24, 1911, in the chapel at Ore Place in Hastings.

Does Christ, in fact, have all the answers? Indeed, Charles, *should* Christ have all the answers?

"In brief, I feel I am in a spot of trouble with my superiors. I recently sent a short manuscript, which I titled *La Vie Cosmique*, to my provincial, Père Claude Chanteur. The manuscript will be distributed among the censors appointed by him. I fear that, at best, I will be censured by them and, at worst, I will be severely disciplined. I fear that I have a love of Christ that can not and will not be understood by the Roman authorities.

"But that is not all. There is worse, my friend, much worse. To be sure, Charles, I have been brought to fear for my life. I sense the distinct possibility of being assassinated by, of all people, fellow-Christians."

I stifled my shock at Teilhard's utterance as the waiter arrived to take our orders. I requested a prime-rib roast (well-cooked in the British manner) and Teilhard opted for the rack of lamb (prepared rare as the French prefer it). I left the choice of wine to Teilhard, in whom I had more confidence in that regard. He read the wine list with as much facility as one reads a newspaper, and selected what turned out to be a pointedly delicious Château Larose-Trintaudon *Haut-Médoc*. Teilhard sampled the wine and, always the teaser, quipped to our befuddled and stiffly-upper-lipped wine-steward, "Arrogant, yet refined". The humorous *entr'acte* did not, however, convincingly mask the anxiety he was feeling.

I assured him not to be concerned about dominating

the evening's conversation; I pledged that I would listen carefully whilst taking my dinner. He nodded a "thank you", and began to describe to me what he considered a potentially vicious threat to his Catholic Church. He opened by speaking of a bilateral—indeed, a trans-Atlantic—religious movement, the most vociferous wing of which was in America but whose philosophical foundation lay in Europe. He described this small yet vigorous group as theologically conservative Protestants whose roots could be found in the Millenarianistic movement that emerged during this century. He told me that what might be called "fundamental Evangelicalism" developed in response to the liberal teachings of the "higher" critics, and was fuelled by the perceived bedlam brought about by Modernism.

Teilhard explained: "Whereas in previous centuries Scriptural revelation had determined how to reason, by the late nineteenth century, reason determined what parts of Scriptural revelation, if any, were to be accepted as true. Also, whereas in previous centuries the divine authority of Scripture had been emphasised, during our period it is *human* authorship that is the focus. Some authors suggest that various parts of Scripture possess various degrees of inspiration, with lower degrees (such as historical details) being capable of error. Other writers go further by totally denying the supernatural character of inspiration.

"Rejection of whatever does not conform to the 'educated mentality', for example, human depravity, Hell, the Virgin Birth and miracles, is explained away by the so-called 'Modernists' as pre-critical thinking. Under the influence of the thinking of both Darwin and Hegel, the Bible can be viewed as a record of the evolutionary development of Israel's (later the Church's) consciousness, rather than God's revelation of Himself to Man.

"My immediate problem, Charles, is that I fall into the 'educated-mentality' category of 'new thinker'. I have indeed been influenced by the scholarship of Darwin and Hegel, and I view Christianity as an evolving system as much as I look upon humankind's physical and mental development as a process in a state of continuous flux. Since I speak freely and publish my writings in those regards, my views have become known by both my Church and the Protestant Evangelical right. I have been warned of disciplinary action by the Church Fathers and I have also been threatened with physical harm. The religion of Pierre Teilhard de Chardin seems to fit no-where and it seems to suit no one. I tend to agree with Marcus Terentius Varro when he said, '*Divina natura dedit agros, ars humana aedificavit urbes.*' [32] The truth is, Charles, that divine *and* non-divine entities influence our world."

My head was swirling from Teilhard's soliloquy. Although I had some experience with Christianity in general and the Roman Church in particular,[33] all of this was

---

[32] "God gave us the fields, humans built the cities." From *De re rustica*. Varro was a Roman scholar who lived during the first century B.C.

[33] Although the literature does not directly address the issue, there are some who believe that Dawson was raised a Catholic.

new to me. "Evangelicalism", "Modernism", "Millenarianism". What were these strange movements and how
did Christendom come to be torn so asunder? Why is the
Catholic Church such an open target?

"Pierre", I said, "let us deal with the most immediate
of your problems right now. You say you feel threatened
bodily. You tell me that you sense the shadow of an
assassin. Who is this assassin, and how can you be pro-
tected from him? I cannot believe that, regardless of your
unorthodox Christian philosophy, someone in your Church
wants to *kill* you. Pierre, in the name of God Almighty!,
who wants to kill you?"

He sipped his wine, looked at me with full face, and
whispered dispassionately, "The Evangelicals."

Teilhard was about to continue his story when a second
bottle of wine (another *Haut-Médoc*) was delivered to our
table by the steward. We were surprised since we had not
placed the order. However, accompanying the wine was
a name-card that read *Arthur Conan Doyle, M.D.* The
steward indicated with a glance a table set in a far corner
of the restaurant. Teilhard and I looked in that direction
and saw the smiling face of a large, moustachioed, and
elegant figure who was sitting enjoying a cigar and
brandy. I asked the steward to invite my old friend to
join us. Doyle's company would serve the dual purpose
of relieving the intensity of Teilhard's mood and affording

me the opportunity of introducing him to one of my closest acquaintances.

"Still looking for 'Ice-Age Man'?" Doyle asked as he approached us.

Then, just as I was about to utter my first words of introduction, Doyle assumed a mock academic posture and exclaimed, "Wait, Charles! I can see immediately that your gentleman-friend is a member of the clergy. A priest. Yes, a Roman Catholic priest at that. By the choice of wine, I would deduce that he is French and rather well-cultured." Realising that Doyle was parodying Sherlock Holmes, Teilhard's expression at long last cracked into a smile, and we all three broke into hearty laughter.

"I am Pierre Teilhard de Chardin, Dr Doyle. Please call me Pierre."

"Delighted to meet you, Pierre. Any friend of Charles' is, by extension, a friend of mine, and my friends call me Conan."

The two shook hands and Doyle, still holding his cigar and snifter in his left hand, sat down to join us.

Conan Doyle is a man's man. Subtract his international renown as the creator of and writer about what is probably the world's most famous fictional detective—and if not that, the world's most famous detective—and the residue still speaks volumes for him. Doyle was born on 22 May 1859, the second child (of ten) and eldest son of Charles Doyle, an assistant surveyor in the Scottish Office of Works. His uncle (Charles' brother) Richard ("Dicky") was one of the most famous artists to work for *Punch*. He designed the magazine's cover, showing Mr Punch's long nose and upturned chin, a most popular image.[34] He also rendered the very first illustrations of Sherlock Holmes and company. A devout Catholic, as was Conan's mother, Mary, Uncle Dicky resigned from *Punch* because of the publication's opposition to the Pope's plan to create a Catholic archbishopric and a dozen bishoprics in England.

To buttress his strong Catholic upbringing, Conan's parents wanted him to be educated by the Fathers, and the boy was accepted without payment by the Jesuit school at Stonyhurst. The hope was that he would use this educational introduction as a springboard for dedicating his life to a career in the Church. Continuing his religious studies, Doyle spent a year at a Jesuit school in Austria, after which—to the dismay of his parents—he made the decision to become a physician. In 1881 he earned his Bachelor of Medicine in Edinburgh.

"What might it be, Pierre, that bonds your friendship with a man such as Charles, who affords the Roman Catholic Church so little succour?" Doyle asked. "I fear that he could taint your faith with his almost incessant talk of Darwin's evolutionism."

"Ironically", Teilhard responded, "it is that very point,

---

[34] . . . which it continued to be for more than a century.

My friend, Arthur Conan Doyle

Conan, that bonds our friendship. I have had an interest
in evolutionary theory since I was a little boy. I see
nothing contradictory in simultaneously being a priest
and a Darwinian. That magic word 'evolution' haunts
my thoughts like a tune. It is to me like unsatisfied
hunger, like a promise held out to me, like a summons
unanswered. Indeed, evolution is a passion for me as

strong as my love of God, for the two are in reality only one."

"But, Pierre, how can you have both God *and* Darwin? Is it not true that the one must preclude the other? In what way can you support both the deterministic[35] account of Creation given in Genesis and the slow, unpredictable evolutionary path from lower organism to Man? Is not evolutionism un-Christian?"

"It is to certain people, Conan. The most commonly asked question is: Is evolution a theory, a system, or a hypothesis? I submit it is much more; it is a general condition to which all theories, all systems, all hypotheses must bow and which they must satisfy henceforward if they are to be entertained as true. Evolution is a light illuminating all facts, a curve that all lines must follow. God cannot create, except evolutively. The evidence for evolution is above all verification, as well as being immune from any subsequent contradiction by experience. My particular problem is that Christianity is supposed to be universalist, yet Christians still cling to a mediaeval cosmogony. Christianity is supposed to be futuristic, but Christians still cling to an extra-terrestrial ideal. Christianity is supposed to be personalistic, but Christians still

---

[35] "Deterministic" in the sense that God made humans the pinnacle of His creative activities. Evolution is not deterministic in that there is no "goal"; what occurs is the result of random genetic mutation. The process has no mechanistic target and no preconceived endpoint.

insist on presenting the Gospel as a moral and juridical precept at the expense of the organic and cosmic splendours included in the Pauline doctrine of Christ recapitulating everything in Himself.

"Conan, my basic propositions are these: one, the cosmos under all its aspects, including Man, is to be understood only as a continuous process of evolution, in which each phase has its distinctive period; two, matter is in principle conscious matter, but it requires a high degree of organisation to enable it to cross the threshold beyond which it can begin to manifest itself as consciousness; three, in matter a dual energy is operative: a tangential energy informing and controlling matter in its normal physico-chemical reactions, and a radial energy by which matter is constituted as progressively higher forms of unity; and four, there is a parallelism between complexity and consciousness."

"I see . . . That is, I think I see, Pierre", Doyle said. "Frankly, I lost my Catholic faith while still a youngster. Upon earning my medical degree I refused to proclaim myself as a Catholic doctor. I must say that that decision created a rift which has never healed between my family and me. In fact, Pierre, I was an agnostic for a period of time. My present interest, however, lies in the spiritualist movement, in support of which I count myself a member of the Psychical Research Society.[36]

---

[36] Doyle joined the Society in 1893.

"I consider spiritualism to be infinitely the most important belief in the world, Pierre, and the particular thing which the human race in its present state of development needs more than anything else. Nothing is secure until the religious basis is secure, and that spiritualistic movement with which I am proud to be associated is the first attempt ever made in modern times to support faith by actual provable fact."

I noted to my two companions with virtual incredulity our circumstance: here were three men, all well-educated, who looked upon Christianity in general and Catholicism in particular from three different perspectives. Teilhard, by far the strongest believer of our trio, was an untraditional member of a most traditional organization; Doyle was a Catholic-*cum*-spiritualist; and I, a disavower of Christianity—indeed, of all supernaturalism. Now that Teilhard had met Doyle, I was convinced that our future conversations would be intellectually animated and exciting.

"I must be leaving now", Doyle said in a somewhat disappointed tone of voice after sipping the last of his brandy, "but I look forward to our sitting down again soon to discuss our various opinions on Christianity, evolution and spiritualism. My only prayer is that the meeting will not be too far in the future. Pierre, it has indeed been a pleasure to meet you. We will see each other again soon, I am sure. And, Charles, any time you need a ride in the area to your Piltdown dig, let me know. I would be happy to motor you there."[37]

I delayed Doyle's departure as he was about to take his leave.

"Before you go, Conan", I requested, "please have a look at this. I received it by post about two weeks ago and have been carrying it in my pocket with the hope of meeting you. It is curious in that it echoes one of your own Sherlock Holmes stories—one I read quite a while ago, perhaps as many as eight or nine years. You will immediately recognise it as having been based on your story, 'The Adventure of the Dancing Men'.[38] It completely perplexes me and I would so appreciate it if you could help explain the mystery."

The envelope I handed to Doyle had nothing on it save my name and address, and a stamp cancelled with a

---

[37] Doyle owned a 20-horsepower Lorraine-Dietrich. He was an avid motorist, having entered in a race called Prince Henry's Tour. The prince was Prussian, the race began in Germany and ended in London after a circular tour of England and Scotland. The British (on whose team Doyle participated) won the race. Doyle was fond of saying that "It is the reliability of car and man which counts, not speed." (Doyle was prescient in his purchase of his automobile: A later model of the Lorraine-Dietrich, the B/3/6, had a 6-cylinder, 3466-cc, 70-horsepower engine—it weighed in at 1.06 tons—and won at Le Mans in 1925 and 1926.) In addition to his active interest in automobile racing, Doyle was an avid billiards player (he reached the third round of an international tournament), a world-class cricket player, and an accomplished heavyweight boxer.

[38] Published in December 1903 in the *Strand Magazine* as the third of a series of stories in a collection called *The Return of Sherlock Holmes*.

London postmark. It contained one sheet of paper on which the following hieroglyphs, and nothing else, were inscribed:

"What might this mean, Conan?" I asked.

"Well, Charles", he answered, with a concerned look on his face, "it is obviously from someone who is rather familiar with my work. I have in my files a complete encoding and decoding scheme for the cipher I used in the story, but there is no telling whether or not this code follows the same pattern. I would have to take it home with me for further study. I will contact you when I have a solution, if, that is, I can discover one."

Teilhard and I shook hands with Doyle, and he left the restaurant.

*   *   *

After Doyle had disappeared into the balmy darkness of the evening, Teilhard turned to me and said, "Charles, he mentioned your Piltdown dig. Could he, by any chance . . . ?

"Yes, Pierre. I am sorry I did not mention it sooner, but Conan knows everything. But we'll talk about that some other time. Now, let us return to *your* predicament", I said with no small measure of immediacy. "You tell me that it is the Evangelicals who are threatening your life. Please tell me more. Who are these people and why do they want to harm you?"

Teilhard began to explain to me the roots and the theology of Christian Evangelicalism. Its origin dates from around the 1840's as a reaction to the liberalism of the German "higher critics" and a subsequent move-ment—anchored in Darwin's theory of evolution—called "Modernism." The Evangelicals viewed themselves as de-fenders of orthodox Christianity (read Protestantism) against those who were attempting to accommodate the faith to the realities of the modern world. Evangelicals stress the verbal and inerrant inspiration of the Bible, which is seen as the final and complete authority for faith and practice. Evangelicalism also preaches a rigorous style of life that eschews alcohol, tobacco, and attendance at places of "worldly amusement" such as the stage and theatre. Teilhard indicated that the Roman Church is a primary target of the Evangelicals.

"Although British anti-Modernists do not distinguish between Evangelicals[39] and Pentecostals[40] as their American counterparts do", Teilhard explained, "each is still an avid opponent of the Catholic Church."

"What specifically do the Evangelicals believe?" I asked.

"There are five basic—that is, fundamental—beliefs:[41] one, Christ is God; two, Christ was born of a Virgin; three, Christ died for Man's sins; four, Christ rose bodily from the dead; and five, Christ will return in bodily form. There are, however, many other beliefs, including the Trinitarian God-head,[42] the reality of Satan, eternal bliss

---

[39] Evangelicals (literally "gospel" Christians) are "born-again" members of their Church. Dating back to the 1720s, Evangelicalism is the common ancestor of religious conservatism and fundamentalism.

[40] Pentecostals (for example, Assemblies of God) are both Evangelical and Fundamentalist (used in the modern sense of the term), but have distinctive beliefs different from other Evangelicals and Fundamentalists. For example, Pentecostals "speak in tongues." And, for the record, the "Charismatics" are *not* Fundamentalists. They are active in many denominations and emphasize direct emotional religious experiences.

[41] These beliefs, or fundamentals, were presented in a series of volumes, called *The Fundamentals*, that were published and circulated between 1910 and 1915. The set of books contained essays written by those who followed the fundamentalist credo and covered a wide variety of subjects.

The term "fundamentalism" was coined in 1920 by Curtis Lee Laws, a Baptist and editor of *The Watchman-Examiner*. He wrote for the July 1, 1920, issue: "We here and now move that a new word be adopted to describe the men among us who insist that the landmarks [i.e., the "fundamentals"] shall not be removed. . . . We suggest that those who still cling to the great fundamentals and who mean to do battle royal for the fundamentals shall be called 'Fundamentalists.' "

[42] That is, the Father, the Son and the Holy Ghost representing a triune God.

and punishment, salvation in grace rather than through good works, and Premillenialism."[43]

"But, is what you just described not part and parcel of the belief system of the Roman Church as well?"

"Yes and no. The Evangelicals argue that there is an intrusion of a Roman fallacy. The Catholic Church teaches that there is only one revelation from God, but it has two sources: the first is written—which is the Bible, and the second is the 'tradition' of the living Church. Here, the Evangelicals say, is an obvious and awesome contradiction. The Bible has been officially endorsed by the Catholic Church as the inspired, infallible Word of God. But then, the Evangelicals say, an adulterant is allowed to intrude which is, in fact, the basis for all Roman Catholic error. The contaminant, they claim, is tradition. The result, they continue, is that the humanly inspired traditions of the Church are not only placed on parity with the genuine Word of God but are actually given precedence over it. According to the Evangelicals, when tradition and God's Word fail to agree, the Roman Church chooses—without fail—to accept their human traditions and reject the true Word of God."

"And how do you—that is, your Church—respond to that?"

"Well, from a strictly Scriptural point of view, I can cite

---

[43] Premillenialism is the belief that Jesus Christ will return before the 1,000-year period of peace. This tenet is held today by very few theologians.

II Thessalonians 2:15, which says, *Therefore, brethren, stand firm, and hold the traditions which you were taught, whether by word, or our epistle.* Actually, Charles, there are two types of tradition. There is first 'Tradition' with a capital 'T', which is Sacred Tradition. Sacred Tradition is the body of teachings of Christ and His Apostles which are not explicitly contained in the Bible but were passed on by Jesus to His Apostles, who in turn passed on these teachings to succeeding generations. Catholics also use the word 'tradition' with a small 't' to mean some action or some thing that has been customary in the Church for a long time."

"In what other areas are the Evangelicals at odds with the Catholic Church?"

"They do not—indeed, cannot—subscribe to the doctrine of Papal Infallibility. Although I also have somewhat of a problem with that precept from a philosophical point of view, the Evangelicals, as always, turn to the Bible for relief. In this case, they deny infallibility by quoting Acts 10:26, wherein Cornelius, a God-fearing man, fell down at Peter's feet, and Peter told him: *Stand up; I myself also am a man.*"

"Are there other differences?"

"Yes, there are many. Some of them are the rôle of the priest in the Church, the Mass and Holy Eucharist, the Confessional, Mary as the Mother of God, the worship of Saints, the Biblical Canon, infant baptism, and Purgatory. The list goes on and on. What the Evangelicals are really saying is that the Roman Church is heretical for not being literalist."

"It seems then, Pierre, that the Evangelicals take the Roman Church—in fact, any religious institution—to task if there is any fluctuation from the literal word of the Bible. The smallest interpretation or wavering from the strait and narrow is anathema to them. In that regard, I can fully understand why the Evangelicals reject the notion of Darwinian evolution. To them it is in diametric opposition to God having created the various life-forms once and forever. But it also seems to me that *any* group that uses the Bible—and Genesis, in particular—as the basis for life's origin would have a problem with the descent of species through modification. How have the Catholic Fathers overcome this seeming contradiction?"

"Well, Charles, it turns out that evolution in principle is not so disturbing for Roman Catholicism as it is for the Protestants. The initial reaction of Rome *was* a strenuous repudiation of evolution—books on the subject by scholars such as Fathers Edward Leroy and John Zahn were withdrawn from circulation by edict. The Vatican Council of 1870 and subsequent encyclicals attacked the new trends in Biblical scholarship. The Modernist movement among Catholic intellectuals was specifically condemned in 1907. However, the new scholarship is now being more favorably received by Rome. This is the result of Pope Leo XIII's Pontifical Biblical Commission's instruction in 1902 that the 'substantial authenticity' of the Pentateuch—that is, the first five books of the Bible— must be taught. The word 'substantial' does not, of course, mean 'literal'. It is this difference that raises the hackles of the Evangelicals. There is a theological war in progress, Charles, and I am being attacked by the Evangelicals, and as it turns out, by my own Church as well."

"All this is understandable, Pierre, but why would the Evangelicals want to *kill* you for the sake of philosophical and doctrinal differences. Is that not somewhat extreme under the circumstances?"

"I have no problem, Charles, with the existence and practice of other belief-systems. However, I do have difficulty with the forced imposition of one's credo on another. Although I am a somewhat unusual Catholic, I am a Catholic nevertheless. I write my opinions about the Roman Church and its dogma for anyone to read or ignore. I do not, however, stand in the street shouting about salvation or the coming end of the world. I do not insult another man's intelligence or assault his privacy with meaningless gibberish about damnation to Hell. Nor do I make it a practice of vilifying other religions. The Evangelicals represent all of that and more. I have taken them to task in my writings and they feel threatened. A major frustration of theirs is that they cannot write me off as some lunatic who espouses a thoroughly unsupportable position. In short, they resent my literacy and my stand against their dogmatic rubbish."

I could see that Teilhard was beginning to reach his pace, and I urged him to continue.

"Here, in brief summary is why I am not enamoured

of the Evangelicals, and why the feeling is mutual. There is a new subset of Evangelicals—call them 'creationists' for want of a better term—who believe in the literal *ex nihilo* fabrication of the universe and all it contains by God. They lend absolute literal credence to the universe having been created in six twenty-four-hour days. They believe that all forms of life created by God can be categorised by immutable—that is, non-evolving—'kinds'. They believe that the Flood as described in Genesis actually happened. That they do not believe in evolution means that they do not believe in scientific progress. The creationists' position about the origin of life and Man can be quickly summarized by two points: One, they believe that the living can never originate from the non-living, just as Pasteur, and Spallanzani before him, demonstrated; and two, that Man can not have descended from an animal, because with the creation of Man's consciousness, something essentially different appeared on the scene."

"But, Pierre, they are correct. The emergence of what is living from what is not living *has* never been observed."

"That may seem true on the surface, Charles, but it is not all there is to it. Each phase in the life-process has a time proper to itself. This means that only during one period of terrestrial evolution were the circumstances—condition of the global sea, the temperature, and so forth—of such a nature that this transition could take place. We cannot rule out the possibility that those circumstances might some day be reproduced in the laboratory."[44]

"But what of the origin of Man, Pierre?"

"Once life had arisen—that is, once it had become visible—it sought different ways in which to evolve.[45] The bifurcation into plant and animal kingdoms must have appeared quickly enough. Attempts to develop further continued in both kingdoms.[46] In the particular case of animals (although this was also true of plants), specialisation took place in order to best fit the organism to a particular niche. The ideal animal would be perfectly designed for its particular biological milieu. However, there is a danger in specialisation. Once an animal becomes over-specialised, it is very difficult, if not impossible, for it to change. If its environment suddenly changes,

---

[44] In 1748 a London scientist, John Needham, appeared to demonstrate proof of the spontaneous generation of life after having observed what he called "little animals" in flasks containing boiled water. Lazzaro Spallanzani contributed to disproving Needham's theory through a series of experiments that were conducted in 1767. Needham recanted the following year.

In 1936 a Russian biochemist named Alexander Ivanovich Oparin described in a book he published that year, *The Origin of Life*, conditions that were likely to have existed on the early Earth and the random chemical and physical processes that were possible in that environment. Seventeen years later, Stanley Miller, using almost the same conditions in his experiments, produced amino acids in his laboratory. He had succeeded in producing proto-life compounds in a test tube.

[45] This is a somewhat teleological statement. Actually, life does not "seek" to evolve since evolution is not goal-directed in that sense. A life form (better term: genetic pool) becomes suitable to a particular environment after experiencing what Darwin called "descent with modification."

[46] This, too, is rather presumptuous.

it may not have enough 'evolutionary time' to make the appropriate morphological adjustments. If it cannot do that, it more than likely will suffer extinction. In point of fact, Charles, as you know, extinction is the rule rather than the exception in the game of life."

Teilhard continued: "Now, the greatest possibilities for evolution in the right direction, so to speak, lay with those animals that had the biggest brains, that is, the apes. Along with brain-power went bipedalism, which freed up use of the hands (and *vice versa*), as well as other adaptations including binocular colour vision. The crucial factor, however, was development of the brain.

"My fear, though, is that the anti-Darwinians will want to invade the public arena with their creationistic rubbish by teaching it in the schools. There is already a movement in the United States in that direction. I can effectively guarantee you, Charles, that some day it will be deemed illegal to teach Darwinian evolution in a school classroom. There are presently very influential political and ecclesiastical communities in America which are in the process of trying to convince the law-makers of the various States to legislate that the teaching of Darwinism be extra-legal.[47] I do not subscribe to such Evangelical rot and I publicly say so. I am prepared to fight the Good War, as it were, against anti-Darwinians, and I am ready

---

[47] One need only be reminded of the Dayton, Tennessee, Scopes "Monkey Trial" of 1925 to see that Teilhard's fear did indeed materialize.

to use all the power available to me in waging that war. The Evangelicals are quite aware of my position, and have warned me to desist or suffer the consequences. I have a small collection of anonymous and threatening letters to prove my point. I will show them to you some day.

"Now, Charles, perhaps you can understand why it is that I am not upset at having been drawn into your little Sussex Man scheme. As much as you back-handedly invited me to join you in your act of reprisal against the scientific community, I recognised that the very same hoax would represent a weapon which I could use against the Evangelicals. One of the greatest terrors that could be foisted upon that community of tyrants is tangible proof that Man has evolved from a lower form which was intermediate to ape-like creatures and modern *sapiens*. Although I do believe that legitimate proof in the form of legitimate fossil remains will someday be presented to the scientific community and to the world at large, the fabrication of 'temporary evidence' of such evolutionary descent will serve very well the purpose at hand. Your scheme presents itself to me as a powerful vehicle for putting the fear of God, as it were, into the most God-fearing Christians on Earth. Your judgement of my character and motivation was very good, Charles. Let us now toast to the success of our newly-founded partnership."

We clinked glasses and drank the last of the wine to which Doyle had so kindly treated us. I then summoned the waiter for coffee and brandies. As I savoured the wonderful aroma of the *Napoléon*, I felt myself swelling with pride and satisfaction over my alliance and friendship with Teilhard. He was, I remember musing, nothing less than unique.

Three days later, on 25 June 1912, I received another cryptic letter in the post. Once again the envelope gave no indication as to the identity of this mysterious "Mr X".[48] And once again it was impossible for me to penetrate the message. Being now Monday, I would not be interrupting Doyle's week-end; so that evening I made an unannounced call at his home, "Windlesham", in Crowborough.

I rapped the heavy brass door-knocker at the entrance to the Doyle residence. When the door opened, I was not surprised to be greeted by a page adorned in a uniform complete with brass buttons and cap, since I had visited Windlesham many times before. The Doyle home is quite large and reflects the life-story as well as style of its master.

---

[48] Interestingly, a "Mr. X" *was* introduced into the body of literature surrounding the identity of the perpetrators. Charles Blinderman relates the story in *The Piltdown Inquest*: "According to [Robert] Essex [Science Master of Uckfield Grammar School, adjacent to Dawson's law office] one of the [Barkham farm] diggers had come looking for Mr. Dawson, who was at the time in court. The visitor had left his bag there, and the clerk had opened it. Inside, he found 'a fossil half-jaw much more human than an ape's and with three molars firmly fixed in it.' The clerk called Essex, who happened to be walking by, into the office and showed him this object. The digger returned and retrieved his bag. The clerk may not have replaced the jawbone. Sometime later, Essex met Robert Kenward [then the tenant at Barkham Manor]. Kenward was looking for the owner of the bag, who was 'distractedly searching for something he had lost.' Essex is cryptic about what this all portends. The owner of the bag, whom Essex names X, apparently was trafficking in jawbones" (p. 115).

I was relieved of my hat by the page and, presently, a lovely wisp of a woman with a most engaging smile entered the hallway and invited me in. Doyle had met her in 1897 and had fallen instantly love. For all my powers of logic, I cannot understand how he could have maintained a Platonic relationship with her until their marriage in 1907, for Jean Leckie Doyle is a beautiful woman.

But Doyle is the consummate gentleman and would never have brought disgrace or dishonour to his first wife Louise. (He had married Louise Hawkins in 1885. She bore them two children: Mary in 1889 and Kingsley in 1892. Unfortunately, Mary died in 1906.) And so, although he was in love with Jean, he refused to divorce Louise. Instead, he and Jean agreed to dwell apart as long as Louise lived. After a long illness, Louise succumbed to tuberculosis during the morning of 4 July 1906.

Jean has soft, brown hair, an exquisite forehead, a long, grave, delicately chiselled face, with sadly reflective, tender eyes that often seem to be looking at something far away. Her nose is straight, her mouth soft, her jawline firm and rounded. Her neck is one of her loveliest features; it is long and slender, and her shoulders slope beautifully. She has a delightful speaking voice, and is a rather well-accomplished opera singer.

"Ah, Charles", she said, "what a pleasant surprise to see you! Do come in. Conan told me that he had met you at the restaurant the other night, and I said to him that we must have you and Hélène here for dinner. How is she, by the way? I haven't see her in such a long time."

"She is just fine, Jean. Funnily enough, we had the same conversation as you and Conan, the difference being that Hélène insisted we have *you* to dinner in Lewes next Friday evening. I fear the worst from her if I cannot return home with an acceptance to our invitation."

"I'm sure we'll be there, Charles. We are so looking forward to seeing Hélène."

With those words, Doyle came into the hallway and said, "I *knew* I heard a friendly voice. Good to see you, Charles. Please come into my study. I have some information in which you may be interested."

We walked up a wide flight of stairs to the landing and turned left into Doyle's office. The place was Spartan in comparison to the rest of the house. His desk was small, barely more than three feet in width. Sitting on it were several stacks of handwritten manuscript, a few books and an ink-well. There were several paintings hanging on walls papered in a floral print pattern, and behind the desk on the left hung a blackboard onto which were pinned photographs of family members. It was difficult to believe that this is all that was materially required to create the Sherlock Holmes canon.

Jean graciously delivered two cups of coffee to the study and with a delicious smile on her face said, "I thought you two boys would like some of this." We thanked her, and she left.

"Conan, were you able to decipher that message?" I asked with anticipation.

"Yes, but with no small degree of difficulty. However, as you know, I enjoy amusements that exercise my powers of logical deduction, and welcomed the opportunity."

The original

Doyle's copy

He then lay two sheets of paper on his desk. One was the original that I gave him; the other looked similar to the first.

"Do you discern a difference between the two copies?" Doyle asked.

After having looked carefully at them, I realised that Doyle's copy appeared to be the mirror-image of the original. "What brought you to rearrange the message in such a way?" I wondered aloud.

"It actually took some time for me to realise that that was the structure required for deciphering the code. At first, I struggled with the message in its original form and got nowhere. It then struck me that I might try the same thing but with the paper turned under-side-up. That brought success."

"But how did you effectuate the decoding? How did you know what to do?"

"Simple. Well, relatively simple, Charles. You were quite correct about 'The Adventure of the Dancing Men'. In it, Holmes is faced with a similar problem. His logic went thus:

> Having once recognised that the symbols stood for letters, and having applied the rules which guide us in all forms of secret writings, the solution was easy enough. . . . As you are aware, E is the most common letter in the English alphabet, and it predominates to so marked an extent that even in a short sentence one would expect to find it most often. . . .
>
> But now came the real difficulty of the inquiry. The order

of the English letters after E is by no means well marked, and any preponderance which may be shown in an average of a printed sheet may be reversed in a single short sentence. Speaking roughly, T, A, O, I, N, S, H, R, D, and L are the numerical order in which letters occur; but T, A, O and I are very nearly abreast of each other. . . .

"Now, unfortunately, your letter did not quite follow the scheme presented by Holmes in the story. However, the general principle still applied. It turned out that E was *not* the most common letter. So I went on the next most common vowel, which is A. *That* was the key to the solution. After no more than several hours' work, during which I tried a variety of permutations and combinations of letter-frequency, I was able to solve the puzzle. However, I can assure you, Charles, that you will not appreciate its contents."

"And pray, Conan, what does it say?" I begged.

"It is devastating, Charles. It says: I KNOW WHAT YOU ARE DOING. I WANT TO HELP. SUSSEX MAN."

I was visibly shaken; Doyle had a frown on his face.

I then said to him: "Conan, I have received yet another message."

I removed from my coat pocket the new message and placed it in front of Doyle. It was enciphered with the same "dancing men", and Doyle immediately began to apply the same procedure he had used for decoding the previous message. He turned the sheet of paper underside-up on his desk and, with great facility, began to write letters of the alphabet below each of the symbols. Within ten minutes, he presented me with the following:

T C E P X E

Y R E V I L E D

T H G I N O T

E G A K C A P F O

G N I N I A T N O C

S C I L E R

N A M X E S S U S

"Expect delivery tonight of package containing relics. Sussex Man."

"*My word!* Conan", I gasped. "I must go home to see what was delivered!"

"Shall I come with you, Charles?"

"No, Conan, not right now. I understand that you and Jean have agreed to join Hélène and me for dinner Friday evening. I'll invite Pierre also, and we can discuss this development."

I ran home without even the courtesy of saying good-night to Jean.

Rushing through the front door, I sped towards my study.

"Charles", Hélène said, "there is a package . . ."

I tore past her.

". . . on the desk in your study."

As a child would do on Christmas morning, I frantically ripped open the package, which was as large as a lady's dress box, but not before I noticed that once again there was no indication on the outside of whom my benefactor might be. I was astounded by the contents when I cleared away the extraneous sawdust packing material.

I could not contain myself.

"Hélène. *Hélène!*" I cried in what must have sounded like a desperate tone, since my wife appeared in an instant.

"What is it, Charles? Whatever is the matter?"

"Hélène, please do me a favour. I will hitch up the horse and carriage. I will take you to the station. From there take the train to Hastings, find Teilhard at Ore Place, and return here with him as quickly as possible. I do not want to alarm you, dear Hélène. This is not a matter of life and death, but it is very important nevertheless. Since it is only half past seven now, I expect that you should arrive back here with Teilhard around ten o'clock. To speed up his response to my request that he accompany you, tell Teilhard that I received a package from 'Sussex Man'. He will understand."

I continued rummaging through the contents of the package when I returned from the station, and found a pot-pourri of treasures. The package contained hippopotamus, beaver, stag, mastodon, and elephant remains, the mixture of which was represented by both bones and teeth. My quick analysis of their origin ran thus: The hippo bone could very well have been of English origin (East Anglia or the Thames terrace), or perhaps from the Continent (the Somme Valley in France), or even from Tunisia, Malta, or Borneo. The elephant bone—a femur, about which more later—could have come from the Thames terrace or the Somme Valley. The *Elphas* molar fragments might have been of Tunisian origin.[49] Clearly,

---

[49] The following items had been "found" at Piltdown as of late June 1912: *Hippopotamus amphibius* (lower premolar and left lower molar), *Mastodon arvernensis* (molar), *Segodon sp.*, since reclassified as *Elephas planiforns* (two molars), *Cervus elephus*, a red deer (antler and proximal end of metatarsal), *Equus sp.*, a horse (left upper molar), and *Castor fiber*, a beaver (lower molar and fourth lower premolar). Also, a variety of eolithic implements were unearthed. And, as we shall see, more human remains were found.

I thought, my benefactor must be a well-travelled and knowledgeable man.

The package also contained a sealed envelope. I opened it carefully and removed the sheet of paper it contained. The note was type-written this time, and read:

I TRUST THIS MATERIAL WILL BE HELPFUL. YOU SHOULD HAVE NO TROUBLE SELECTING FROM AMONG IT. YOU SHOULD ALSO HAVE NO PROBLEM PREPARING IT FOR INTERMENT.

YOUR SECRET IS SAFE.

†

I was dumbfounded. *Who, other than Teilhard and Doyle, could have known?* How did he come to learn of our plan? Where did he obtain the contents of the package? How could his timing be so perfect? What did the signature mean?

I decided to forego consideration of these questions and continue examining the contents of the box.

I was anxious for Teilhard's arrival; I wanted to show him the most precious specimen of the lot.

Hélène delivered Teilhard much sooner than I had expected. This was fortunate, since to calm my excitement, I was sipping my third brandy when they arrived. I thanked my wife for the favour she had performed, and likewise showed gratitude to Teilhard for his quick response to my request. He accepted my offer of a brandy and asked simply, "What hath 'Sussex Man' wrought?"

While Teilhard was catching his breath from what he described as a frantic carriage ride from the station, I related to him my receipt of the "Dancing Men" notes, as well as my meeting of only several hours ago with Doyle. I then showed him the note that had been included in the package. As if to substantiate my own bewilderment of the package's mysterious source, Teilhard asked with awe, "How could anyone have known?"

"I do not know", was the only response I could offer.

"Well, Charles", said Teilhard, "let's do it. Let us see what our benefactor has sent."

I handed the prize specimen to Teilhard and asked him to open it, at which point he untied the string and carefully unfolded the heavy brown butcher's-type paper. He laid the whole on my desk with the contents unveiled.

"This is *astounding*, Charles!" he cried. *"This is absolutely astounding!"*

I nodded agreement, for sitting atop the unfolded paper was the right half of a hominid-like mandible.

"Can you identify this jaw, Pierre?" I asked.

"I am not an anatomist, Charles, but I will certainly give it a try."

"One need not be a student of anatomy to see the significance of this specimen."

"Well", he responded, while carefully turning it through his hands, "it is certainly not of human origin, Charles."

"And how do you know that?"

"It is not built like that of a human."

"Specifically, Pierre, *specifically*", I pleaded. *"How* is it not human?"

"I see morphological differences in three areas. First, Charles, the jaw possesses no symphysis—it has no chin. Second, the canine, relative to the other teeth, is larger than that of a human, in addition to which there is evidence of a diastema into which the upper canine would fit. And third, the condyle of this jaw would not articulate with the cranium as in a human because it emerges from the ramus at the wrong angle.[50] My guess is it's a chimpanzee, or an evolutionary relative of the chimpanzee."

---

[50] The following figure illustrates Teilhard's analysis of the jaw fragment:

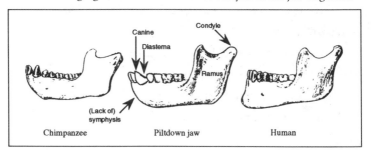

At first glance, a chimpanzee's jaw resembles a human jaw. This is because they are related in form and function as a result of common ancestry. However, humans do not possess the large canines of their anthropoid cousins, which are used by those animals for defense and display. Humans

"Pierre, I must say that you know your anthropoid anatomy very well. This is, indeed, not a human jaw. I would wager every shilling and penny I possess that it belonged at one time to an orang-utan."

"*Orang-utan?* Why, the only known habitat of those animals is Borneo. Charles, how could you have come into possession of an orang-utan's jaw?"

I shrugged off Teilhard's question with a sigh.

"Before we examine the contents in earnest", I said, "please sit down, and I will fill you in on a few details."[51]

---

do, however, have a chin, the survival benefit of which condition is not yet completely understood. (Perhaps the chin is in some way related to diet and the ability to speak.) The condyle forms a less severe angle with the ramus in humans than it does in apes. This may also be related to diet and speech. (Illustration after Dawson and Woodward, 1913, Geological Society)

[51]Since Dawson's narrative will now turn toward a discussion of how the Piltdown remains were prepared for interment, it would be a good time to look at a reconstruction of the skull based on the fragments that were found. This is done in the interest of becoming familiar with the anatomical nomenclature. The reconstruction pictured below is from Grafton Elliot Smith, *The Evolution of Man* (London. Oxford University Press, 1924).

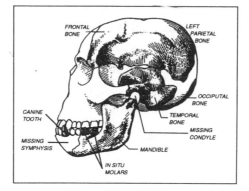

I began to relate to Teilhard the particulars of the "finds" I had made in 1911. I told him that I had procured a rather complete human calvaria, which was to be the centre-piece of the fraud. I also obtained other artifacts, including the lower premolar of a hippopotamus.

"I needed the hippo tooth", I explained, "as corroborating evidence for what I wanted to be interpreted as great age for the skull. However, having already examined a number of other cranial specimens, I realized that my skull and hippo tooth were not of appropriate colouration to be represented as convincingly ancient. Somehow, they had to be stained. Using a ploy of wanting to better preserve the fossils, I asked my friend Samuel Woodhead, who is Public Analyst for East Sussex and Hove, as well as an agricultural analyst and competent chemist, how I might prevent damage to the specimens by hardening them. He suggested that I dip the bone and tooth in a solution of potassium bichromate.[52] This was an efficacious endeavour, since the specimens achieved a rich mahogany colouration, almost precisely that of legitimate fossils found in local ferruginous deposits.

"Having achieved success with the potassium bichromate, I then proceeded to stain in like manner the left

---

[52] Also called potassium dichromate, $K_2Cr_2O_7$, it is made by adding sulfuric acid (H_2SO_4) to potassium chromate (K_2CrO_4).

frontal, left temporal and occiputal bones to match the left parietal.

"Now I also had an eolith which I dipped into my 'ageing solution'. It was precisely the stone tool you found on the second of June when we were at the Barkham farm with Smith Woodward.[53] Since I had previously tested the elixir on other stones recovered from the gravel-pit, I knew that even a trained eye would have trouble seeing through my ploy. My suspicion in that regard was confirmed when even you, a competent geologist, did not notice anything untoward. I have collected some similar stones, which are not manufactured tools, on which to experiment. Since you have studied chemistry from a more formal standpoint than I, perhaps you will be interested to see how this procedure works."

"By all means, yes, Charles", Teilhard said excitedly.

I prepared a mixture of potassium bichromate in a glass bowl. I then dropped a few of pieces of Wealden stone into the liquid and stirred with a glass mixing rod. After a few minutes, I removed the stones and allowed them to dry, during which time they achieved a rich, red-coloured patina.

"All that has to be done, Pierre", I said, "is identify the precise ratio of chromate to acid in order to achieve

---

[53] Dawson is referring here to the E606 implement.

the proper colouration. Alternatively, since potassium bichromate is soluble in water, we can vary the dying properties by controlling the amount of water mixed in."

"This is fascinating, Charles."

"Yes, indeed. What I would like to do now is prepare for deposit some of the articles contained in the 'Christmas-in-June' package I received today. I am particularly interested in working on the orang-utan's jaw. It will require some preparation—that is, Pierre", I said with a grin, "some poetically-licensed morphological revision. It will also need staining before it will be of any use to us. Are you interested in working through the night with me?"

"As it says in Isaiah 21:5, *Prepare the table.*"

The mandible required quite a bit of meticulous work. It would have to be altered so as to suggest tantalising clues. I knew that, as Teilhard had pointed out, the major differences between human and anthropoid jaws lay in the structure of the condyles, the symphysis and the canine teeth. In addition, because of the simian diet of rough vegetation, the molars would not be worn as they are in humans—the occlusal surfaces would have to be made flatter. Those were then the evidences that would have to be either covered up, removed from or added to the orang-utan jaw.

I retrieved a sharp knife, a small hammer, a file and a pliers from my desk drawer and began to explain to Teilhard how I was going to accomplish the modification.

I drew the following diagram and showed it to him:[54]

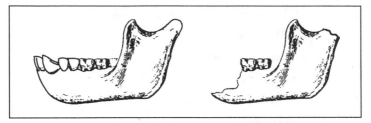

[54]Modified from Dawson and Smith Woodward (1913).

Explaining the plan of attack, I said: "As you can see, Pierre, there are three major alterations that must be effected.[55] First, we must remove the condyle in order to

---

[55]This illustration shows what Dawson set out to accomplish:

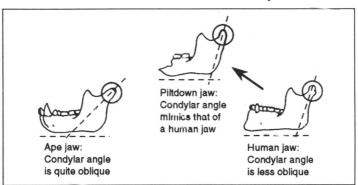

In an ape (such as an orangutan), the angle that the base of the jaw makes with the condyle is very oblique. Had the condyle remained attached to the jaw, the source would have been obvious. By removing the condyle Dawson at least opened up the possibility that it would be reconstructed as if it had come from a hominoid jaw, that is, the condylar angle would be made to be more acute. Dawson's ploy worked. Smith Woodward eventually reproduced the jaw with a human condylar structure, thus giving birth to the Piltdown jaw.

obscure the angle of insertion of that bit of anatomy into the cranium. If we leave the condyle in its present condition, the angle of articulation of the mandible with the skull will become evident, and this will betray the anthropoid source of the jaw. Second, we must remove the symphysis to hide the absence of a chin. Of course, the lower incisors, the canine and the two premolars will disappear along with the chin. I suggest we also remove the rear-most molar. And third, we must refashion the surfaces of the remaining two molars. They must be made flat, as in an adult ape.

"Finally, we will stain with potassium bichromate the product of our artistry to make it match the colouration of indigenous Piltdown pit contents."

I had to exercise an inordinate amount of care in preparing the mandible since it was the only one I had and there was no way I could contact "Mr X" if it were ruined. I decided to amputate the condyle first because, if the job were botched, it would mean only that more of the condyle would have to be removed, and this would not disturb the over-all effect of eliminating witness to the angle of articulation with the skull.

I did not want to saw off the condyle because that would have left a scar and a surface that would betray shenanigans. The edge had to appear naturally broken and somewhat worn. With that in mind, I sketched with a pencil an irregular, closed line around the condyle which defined how I wanted it severed. I then carefully scored the bone with

my knife, using the pencil line as a guide. The bone had
to be scored rather deeply because it was not so brittle as I
had expected (my guess is that it was several hundred years
old).[56] In fact, the mandible was not even completely fossilized. At a point where Teilhard agreed that the scoring was
deep enough, I placed the mandible on several layers of
folded cloth and, with Teilhard securing the one end of the
jawbone with his weight leaning one hand upon the other,
I said a silent prayer (Teilhard glanced up to the heavens),
and sharply struck the end of the condyle with the hammer's
head. The condylar fragment flew from the ramus and
bounded across the room as the perspiration was shaken
from my brow to the floor.

"I now know the stress a diamond-cutter feels every
day of his life", I said to Teilhard with a smile as I wiped
my brow with a handkerchief. "I could never do that sort
of work for a living."

Upon examining the stump of the ramus, we agreed
that it needed improvement since the break was too keen
for it to have occurred naturally. I went into the kitchen
and purloined Hélène's steel meat-pounder, using it carefully to aggravate the surface of the ramus from which
the condyle was rent. After several minutes of nervous
discourse, Teilhard and I agreed that there was virtually
no room for improvement without the threat of destroying
the piece.

---

[56] It was about 500 years old.

It was already half past one in the morning and we felt exhausted. "Brandy?" I asked.

Teilhard's gesture of assent afforded us the opportunity for some relaxation. Five minutes later, during which period not a word was said between us, a mutual smile and nod was the signal to continue our escapade.

"Do we want to save the incisors, the canine and the premolars?" I asked, knowing that they would fall off along with the symphyseal section.

"Well", Teilhard answered, "why not try to remove one of the premolars with the pliers? If it fails and we need the other premolar, we can always have another brandy and think about how surgery on *that* one might be performed." We both snickered. "On the other hand", he continued, "if the premolar can be extracted without incident, we will have the option of interring another artifact. I would suggest, however, that if you are going to play dentist with the mandible, gauze should be wrapped around the jaws of the pliers in order to protect the tooth as much as possible."

Teilhard's suggestions accepted, I prepared the pliers, gripped the first premolar and gently pulled it, using a rocking motion. I felt the tooth begin to loosen, eased up on the pressure, and neatly separated the intact premolar from its socket.

"It will be a cold day in Hell, sir", Teilhard said, "before I make an appointment for the services of Charles Dawson, D.D.S."

We were similarly quite successful in dissociating the

symphysis from the body of the jawbone. Next, I treated the newly-exposed surface of the mandible with Hélène's meat-pounder. Now all that remained of the mechanical processing of the bone was to render the two remaining *in situ* molars flat so they resembled those of an adult ape. I had a very fine metallic nail-file which would serve the purpose well. With Teilhard gripping the jaw firmly in both hands, I began to file down the cusps of the first tooth. Within seconds, Teilhard shrieked: *"Stop!"*

"We have a problem, Charles. The fact that there are still somewhat well-defined cusps on the teeth indicates that we are dealing with the jaw of a rather young orang-utan. It is true, is it not, that the cusps wear down with use as the animal ages? Wouldn't we be opening the door to exposure by planting a young mandible with 'old' teeth?"

"Under ordinary circumstances, the answer would be yes, Pierre. However, this specimen, I would think, belonged to a young ape, and a fairly large one at that. He has a full complement of teeth and, except for the molars, they look like those of a mature animal. Have no fear, Pierre. A little adulteration will not hurt this adolescent."

Teilhard gripped the mandible again, and I began filing the surface of the forward molar very tenderly, first this way and then that, in a cross-hatched manner. I did this to eliminate as much as possible any file-marks.[57]

---

[57] This ploy did not work. File marks were eventually discovered on the surface of the teeth. And there is worse: read on.

After several minutes of work, it appeared to each of us upon inspection that the tooth had belonged to an adult orang-utan. All that remained now was to file the second tooth.

Teilhard regripped the jawbone, and I began to file anew. I felt more confident this time, and was able to work the tooth down a bit more quickly. After not too much time, I was finished and took the piece from Teilhard for inspection.

"*BLOODY HELL!*"

Teilhard jumped. "What is it, Charles?"

I was rather angry and quite embarrassed.

"Look, Pierre. *Look.* I've *really* bungled things now!"

With a false sense of security in my orthodontic prowess, I had inadvertently filed the two teeth down in different planes. I felt like a blithering idiot, it being now quite impossible to mend the error because in so doing too much of one tooth would have to be removed to even out the occlusal surfaces.[58]

"Well, Charles", Teilhard said in a tone of voice de-

---

[58] Here is an illustration of what happened:

signed to calm me, "it looks like it is time for another brandy."

We decided, however, that leaving well enough alone (in a manner of speaking) was the path to take. Thus, we agreed that we would leave the jaw as it was and hope for the best. I mentioned to Teilhard that I would like him to accompany me to the Piltdown pit-site this week-end so that we could deposit the bogus jaw and other artifacts among the gravel. Teilhard said with disappointment that he would have to beg off my invitation because he was otherwise engaged.

I told him that I expected Smith Woodward would attend my excursion to Piltdown, and that, in addition to the jaw, I hoped we would "recover" several more cranial fragments, along with some of the assorted bones and implements that were sent by "Mr X". I assured him that I would give him a full report when I saw him next.

"But what of the canine?" Teilhard inquired.

"Based on tonight's debacle with the jaw's molar teeth, I think we should reserve judgement about how to handle that until we are more rested and have a more reliable plan."

"Also, Charles", Teilhard said somewhat nervously, "notwithstanding the kindness of an anonymous benefactor supplying us with excellent specimens, it is clear— indeed, *dangerous*—that somebody else is aware of our charade. Unless we learn his identity, we are threatened with exposure. We must find out who he is."

Dangerous?, I thought; why *dangerous?* The word stuck in my mind.

"Yes, Pierre. For that reason, I have invited Conan Doyle to join Hélène and me for dinner on Friday evening. It would be helpful if you could also attend, so that the three of us can decide how we will handle that development."

"I shall be there", Teilhard assured me.

"As for now, Pierre, it is a quarter to four, and I think we should get some sleep. I am going directly to bed, but if you like, have another brandy and show yourself to the guest-room. I bid you a restful night."

The next morning, at a late breakfast prepared for us by Hélène, I told Teilhard that since I was meeting Smith Woodward on the coming week-end, I must deposit the mandible to-day or to-morrow. He apologised again that he would not be able to join me, but wished me luck with the interment and eventual disinterment. He departed soon after our meal.

Doyle and Teilhard arrived at my home on Friday within three minutes of each other, and neither later than five minutes past the agreed-upon rendezvous. Doyle and his wife Jean came first, having travelled by motor from Crowborough. Teilhard was delivered by cab from the train station.

Hélène and I greeted them at the door. Surprisingly

enough, Doyle and Teilhard each presented us with a gift of two bottles of *Haut-Médoc*. Doyle said his wine was to honour seeing Teilhard again; Teilhard mentioned that he was returning the favour granted us by Doyle when we saw him at the Crowborough restaurant. Jean presented Hélène with a most beautiful selection of flowers chosen from her garden.

After the greetings and exchange of gifts, Doyle patted his sizeable stomach and said, "Well, now, I'm as hungry as a bear, Hélène, and I hear you are a wonderful cook!" Hélène smiled and responded, "Thank you, Conan. I hope you will enjoy your dinner." Then she added, "Why don't you all have a cocktail and I'll show Jean the secret to my culinary success." Jean and Hélène went to the kitchen, and Doyle, Teilhard and I retired to my study, where I poured three whiskys.

"Gentlemen", I said after our toast, "last night I planted the mandible Pierre and I worked on earlier this week. Smith Woodward will be here tomorrow at noon to join me for a brief luncheon, after which we will go to the gravel-pit to 'discover' it. Let us hope our good Arthur has the fortune to find it without undue exertion."

"*Here, here!*"

"Now we have two serious problems to discuss", I continued. "The first is: Who is this mysterious Mr X who is sending me those curious notes? And the second is . . . well, I'll let Teilhard explain the second, since it concerns him directly."

Teilhard briefly related the tale of his fear of assassination for us, with Doyle listening very intently. When he had finished, he removed a piece of paper from his coat pocket and handed it to Doyle, who read it with a spasm of shock and passed it to me. I, too, was stunned. The note read:

HERETIC TEILHARD:
    YOU LIVE FOR SATAN AND WILL DIE IN THE NAME OF GOD ALMIGHTY. MAY YOUR BONES BURN FOR ETERNITY IN THE INFERNO OF HELL WITH THOSE OF YOUR SUSSEX MAN.

                                                    †

"What does the signature mean, Pierre?" I asked.

"Well, they are clearly Christians", Teilhard said with a nervous smile.

"Yes", said Doyle, "and I would wager it is those new Evangelicals by the angry and intolerant tone of the note."

I then showed Doyle and Teilhard the note that had been included with the package of relics. Their eyes immediately went to the signature.

I heard Teilhard blurt out "Holy Mother of Jesus!" under his breath.

I asked the obvious question: "*Is the same person or persons who sent me the relics also threatening Pierre with his life?*"

"Apparently so", Doyle responded with tightened lips.

"Why would anybody want to support the discovery

of evidence for human evolution and at the same time threaten with assassination the person who finds it?" Teilhard asked.

"I cannot understand it", I conceded.

"I confess that I do not know either", said Doyle. "It is quite curious. However, something must be done about it. We shall find and confront the responsible party, for I am convinced he means serious business and that this no practical joke. I can assure you that the threat to Pierre is not empty."

"This farce of ours is turning out to be rather an adventure, and an altogether dangerous one at that", Teilhard interjected. "Perhaps we should abandon it, confess our sins, and cut our losses."

"*No!*" I said. "We . . . er, I . . . have a reputation to maintain. I refuse to reward the conceit of Academia with my humiliation! And to put my mind at rest, I must ask both of you once and for all, *Are we still together in this caper?*" I turned towards Teilhard: "Pierre, are we still together?"

"Proverbs 18:24 teaches us—*there is a friend that sticketh closer than a brother*. You can count on me, Charles."

"And you, Conan? Will you help us resolve this conundrum?" I pleaded anxiously.

Doyle remained quiet with chin against chest, silent in thought, fondling his glass of whisky.

I repeated with a naked sense of immediacy: "I implore you, my good man, *you must help us!*"

Doyle lifted his head, glanced first at Teilhard and

then at me. With a warm smile, he finally assuaged my concern: "Gentlemen, in the celebrated words of Sherlock Holmes himself, *The game is afoot!*"

It would now appear an appropriate point in this reminiscence to speak of Smith Woodward in more detail. He is one of the very small handful of qualified men of science whose studies are respected and whose notions on the evolutionary origin of *Homo sapiens* are granted any authority. Most of the academic activity in that arena centres on France, Germany, America and, of course, England. There are highly vociferous and strongly opinionated voices within each of those quarters. As perhaps the most accomplished paleo-ichthyologist of our time, Smith Woodward's views are very closely attended to.

Arthur Smith Woodward, my precise contemporary (we were both born in 1864),[59] is the son of a Macclesfield, Cheshire, dye manufacturer. He had and continues to enjoy an exemplary career and reputation in the natural sciences. It was he who, in 1891, first described the *Plagiaulax* tooth that I unearthed in the Weald. We also communicated about the *Dipriodon* find discovered by Félix Pelletier, Teilhard and myself in 1909.

A young Arthur (he was merely eighteen years of age)

---

[59] Smith Woodward and Dawson were also coincidentally admitted to the Geological Society of London on the same day in 1885.

Arthur Smith Woodward, my precise contemporary

was appointed as an assistant in the Geological Department of the British Museum (Natural History) before he had even completed the requirements for his university degree. Between 1889 and 1901 he prepared and published a four-volume catalogue of the Natural History Museum's vast fossil fish collection. In 1889 he was awarded the Wollaston Medal by the Geological Society, which was followed in 1896 by the prestigious Lyell Medal. He was promoted to Keeper of the Royal Geological Society in 1901,[60] after having served almost ten years

---

[60] . . . and remained so until 1924.

as its Assistant Keeper. That same year, he was elected a Fellow of the Geological Society (F.G.S.). His published work includes the *Catalogue of British Fossil Vertebrata* (1890) and *Outlines of Vertebrate Palaeontology* (1898). Although somewhat stiff, formal and strait-laced, his intelligence and propensity for hard work cannot be denied.

On Saturday, 30 June 1912, Smith Woodward arrived at my home in Lewes, as planned, for a light luncheon. Neither spirits nor wine were served by Hélène. Although my wife and I had known Smith Woodward for years, there was somewhat more formality and less small talk than should otherwise have been the case. Even under the circumstance of long acquaintance, an air of detachment still accompanied him.

"Have you studied the cranial fragments and the eolith we and Teilhard found earlier this month?" I asked whilst we were having our second cup of coffee.

"Yes, I have, Charles. The three parietal fragments join together quite well and I concluded that they were definitely parts of the same cranium. In addition, I was able to join the broken edge of the occipital you found with yet another fragment. The pieces of the puzzle are beginning to fit together quite well. I am starting to believe with greater security that we have discovered something very important."

"Are you in a position to characterise the skull yet?"

"Not with absolute specificity, Charles. However, my

preliminary sense is that we are in possession of extremely archaic human remains that, based on the deposits in which they were found, date to the Pliocene/Pleistocene boundary."

"You mean, Arthur, that the skull is one million years old?"[61] I asked.

"It appears so. If that is the case, we have identified not only the first Englishman, Charles, but the earliest human-like creature in the world. England shall indubitably be privileged by this discovery of ours. In that regard, I should not be so presumptuous as to assume that I can freely share in the recognition as a discoverer of the remains, for it is really you and Teilhard who should possess that honour."

"Not at all, Arthur", I stated matter-of-factly. "I can assure you that your name will be forever associated with Sussex Man."

We rode by carriage to the Barkham farm and walked to the gravel-pit, where we were met by Chipper, the Kenwards' pet goose, whose curiosity about our activities was to keep him constantly under foot. It was by now almost two in the afternoon and the pressure of the summer heat and accompanying humidity could be felt. We

---

[61] The Plio-Pleistocene boundary is now thought to be 2 million years before the present.

removed our digging tools from the carriage and carried them to the site in a canvas bag.[62]

"Well, Charles", Smith Woodward asked, "where shall we look this time?"

"I'll peruse this area over here", I said. "Why don't you continue searching the area where I found the skull fragments earlier this month? Perhaps other remains that I may have missed are still buried in the vicinity."

---

[62] The following diagram of the Piltdown site appeared in Henry F. Osborn, "The Dawn Man of Piltdown, Sussex," *Natural History* 21 (November–December 1921).

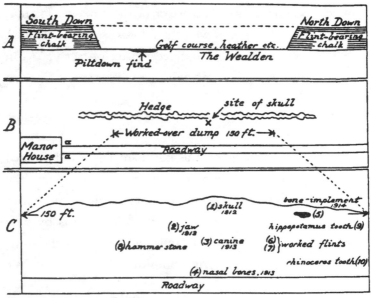

(A) shows a cross-sectional view between the North and South Downs, the area that contains the pit (the golf course still exists); (B) is a bird's-eye view of the pit area in relation to Barkham Manor; (C) is an overhead view indicating the position and dates of some of the finds. (Map by Henry Fairfield Osborn, courtesy *Natural History*)

We searched throughout the whole of the afternoon with no results. I was becoming a bit concerned about Smith Woodward not finding the mandible, although he was rummaging in a circle centred on the site where the skull fragments were discovered, within a radius of no more than two feet. I was wondering whether I would be able to benefit from the "legitimacy" of Smith Wood-ward's making the find himself when, just as I was ready to cry off, he turned towards me and shouted: "Charles! *Charles, I have found something!*"

And, indeed, he had; for there lay, partially exposed, the anterior end of the ruddy-coloured mandible no more than twelve inches from where the skull-bones had been found. Underneath my feigned excitement I breathed a long sigh of relief because the day had almost come to an end and there was virtually no work-time remaining.

I reeled around and faced Smith Woodward. "What is it, Arthur? What have you found?"

"It appears to be a mandible. *I think we've found the mandible!*"

I removed from the canvas bag a small trowel, a den-tist's pick, a tooth-brush and a soft-bristled paint-brush, and—ever so gently—Smith Woodward began the pro-cess of removing the jaw from its two-day-old hiding place. He deliberately left a thin margin of soil deposit around the fragment, and was able after about twenty minutes to extract the piece.

"This is wonderful, Charles! Although the mandible is

incomplete, it appears that it does contain two molars, a very serendipitous occurrence. With your permission, I should like to take the jaw to my laboratory, remove the earth surrounding it, and study it carefully. It would be quite remarkable, Charles, if this mandible fit the cranium."

"Be my guest, Arthur. There is not a person in the world other than you whom I would trust with the piece."

Smith Woodward carefully wrapped the jaw fragment in several layers of gauze and placed the small package in a leather carrying-bag. Although I had invited him to join Hélène and me for dinner that evening, he begged off that proposal in favour of returning as quickly as possible to London. Needless to say, I did not discourage him.

I delivered Smith Woodward by carriage to the station, whence he embarked on a train ride to London. He told me that he would contact me as soon as he had any information about the relationship between the skull-bones and the mandibular fragment.

As I was returning home alone in my carriage, I savoured a rush of well-earned self-aggrandisement.

According to plan, then, Teilhard and I had fabricated a composite ape/human lower-jaw fragment. My hope, of course, was that the missing parts of the mandible (the condyle and the symphysis, in particular) would be reconstructed to demonstrate evolutionary intermediacy of the

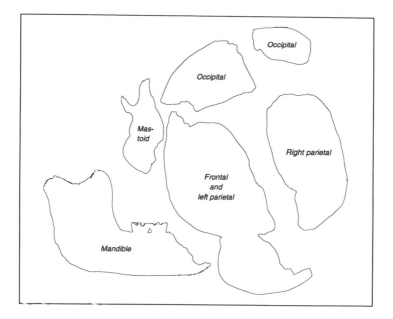

Occipital

Occipital

Mas-
toid

Right parietal

Frontal
and
left parietal

Mandible

jaw between ape and human. The drawing above[63] shows
the cranial material which Smith Woodward had in his
possession as of 1 July 1912.

All I could do at this juncture was await his restoration
of the skull and pray for the best.

The interlude between 30 June and 18 December 1912
(the latter being the date on which Smith Woodward and

---

[63] Adapted from photographs in the Palaeontology/Mineral Library, British
Museum (Natural History).

I made our formal presentation to the Royal Geological Society in London) was filled with frantic activity. While Smith Woodward attended to the reconstruction and characterisation of the skull, I busied myself by preparing a paper designed to address the geology of the area. My plan was to use a geological description and analysis as the foundation for dating the finds. I felt confident that I had placed the bones and other artifacts in the appropriate beds of soil and gravel.

During this five and a half month period of time, Smith Woodward and I were also inundated with voluminous correspondence from members of the scientific community. The flurry of letter-writing originated not only from men belonging to the Geological Society, but also from other scientific associations, as well as the universities. I must say that the brisk interest in the Piltdown remains was gratifying, but it was also somewhat of a nuisance. The letters simply did not stop coming. This was the direct result of a news leak which, on 19 November 1912, I made anonymously to the press.[64] There was also a flurry

---

[64] On November 21, 1912, the *Manchester Guardian* reported about Piltdown Man that "There seems to be no doubt whatever of its genuineness, and more than a possibility of its being the oldest remnant of a human frame yet discovered on this planet." The press learned through the leak that the bones were found in "a gravel pit on the site of an old river bed," and that "a gentleman—a solicitor by profession . . . realised the importance of the discovery [and] collected the fragments . . ." When Smith Woodward was approached by reporters, he told them "to be patient" and wait for the meeting of the Geological Society to be held in December.

of letter-writing activity among members of the Society themselves.

Examples of the correspondence follow. The letters clearly reflect the excitement that was generated by the discoveries.

On November 23, *The New York Times* published the following story, reprinted here in its entirety:

PLEISTOCENE SKULL FOUND IN ENGLAND

Scientists Greatly Interested in a Discovery in Sussex— Details Not Yet Made Public.

IS MILLIONS OF YEARS OLD

As Early as Any Human Relic Found in Europe— A Lower Type Than the Neanderthal Specimen.

Special Cable to *The New York Times*.

LONDON, Nov. 23.—An important prehistoric find in England is causing great excitement among scientists generally, and anthropological students in particular. While excavating in Sussex workmen unearthed the fragments of a human skull, which are now being pieced together. The detailed description is withheld until Dec. 18, when it will be given at a meeting of the Geological Society.

Experts, however, declare that the skull is that of a paleolithic man, and undoubtedly the earliest evidence of man in this country, dating from the beginning of the pleistocene period.

It was found in association with bones of one of the most ancient types of elephant. The stratum in which it lay was the beach of a very old river bed. The skull belongs roughly to the same age as the famous Heidelberg skull and is quite as early as anything which has been found in Europe.

The skull resembles the Neanderthal specimen, but belongs to a much lower and even more primitive type of mankind than that. Before this discovery the earliest skull found in England was one dug up near Ipswich last year, but the conditions of the Ipswich find leave a loophole for doubt.

There is no doubt, it is said, about the geological age of the Sussex skull. Experts will not venture an opinion as to the date of the Sussex man, but he probably lived millions of years ago.

William Boyd Dawkins[65] *to Smith Woodward (6 October 1912)*:
". . . Concerning your wonderful find—I think that the absence of well defined hollows for the reception of the convolutions of the brain, on the inner wall of the skull is of first rate importance."

Edwin Ray Lankester[66] *to Smith Woodward (27 October 1912)*: "I have been thinking of nothing else but that splendid human fossil all day. . . . It seems to me that it would be worth spending thousands on this—a regular systematic and complete sifting of every hatful of gravel in the neighbourhood [of the Piltdown find]."

Arthur Keith[67] *to Smith Woodward (2 November 1912)*: "I should very much like to have a glimpse of that wonderful find—of which rumours have reached me from time to time. It bucks me up to think England is yielding up trumps and that the specimens have reached the right hands—send me a postcard when I may come."

James Reid Moir[68] *to Smith Woodward (12 November 1912)*: "I have been thinking a great deal about that wonderful find of yours since you so kindly showed it to us, and wondering as to the age of the human remains."

---

[65] Dawkins (1837–1929) was professor of geology at Owens College from 1874 to 1908. Smith Woodward was a former student of his.
[66] Lankester (1847–1929) was Director of the British Museum and Keeper of Zoology at South Kensington from 1898 to 1907. He championed Smith Woodward's interpretation of the Piltdown finds.
[67] Keith (1866–1955) was Conservator of the Hunterian Museum of the Royal College of Surgeons. He was knighted in 1921.
[68] Moir (1879–1944) was an Ipswich businessman.

Despite the mountainous correspondence (there were dozens of letters written back and forth during the five months following Smith Woodward's disinterment of the mandible), we managed to prevent more news getting to the press. In fact, we informed the reporters that they must wait until 18th December for additional and more complete information.[69]

Needless to say, I was bubbling with pride and satisfaction that the Sussex Man had begun to receive such spontaneous attention and active interest.

However, the Fourth Estate was not the only party who was privy to the finds.

On 15th October I received at home the following anonymous letter (post-marked London):

IN RESPONSE TO YOUR HEATHEN APOSTASY, MAY THE INFINITELY MERCIFUL GOD OF GRACE LOOSE HIS WRATH UPON YOU AND YOUR FAMILY FOR SEVEN TIMES SEVEN GENERATIONS. IT IS FROM HIM AND HIM ALONE THAT THE MIRACLE OF LIFE CAN COME AND HAS COME.

†

And several days later:

---

[69] Based on a letter from Smith Woodward to Dawkins dated November 25, 1912.

ETERNAL DAMNATION IN HELL, HERETIC DAWSON!
MAY YOU BURN FOREVER IN SATAN'S INFERNO!

†

And yet again:

DIE, HERETIC DAWSON! DIE IN THE NAME OF JESUS!

†

These three letters, having the same cruciform signature as the others, were ominously reminiscent of the anonymous and forbidding note that Teilhard had shown to Doyle and me.

And, although keeping my feelings to myself at the time, I must admit that I was rather unnerved by these communications. The time had come for me to contact Conan Doyle to see if he was making any progress with his detective work.

Doyle visited me a fortnight later, on 2nd November, to apprise me of the progress he had made in regard to his investigation of the threatening letters Teilhard and I had received. We had fish and chips at the local pub. Being Sunday evening, The Lamb was quite empty and Freddie, the piano-player, had the day off. It was very quiet; in fact, Doyle and I had the whole place to ourselves. Doyle's first words to me were, "Charles, we've roused a storm that we may not be able to contain. Any further action we take for the sake of continuing the hoax may well exacerbate the situation. I was correct when I suggested that the circumstances could hold a great deal of danger."

I asked him to explain as we dined.

"Two weeks ago", he began, "I travelled to London to compete in the Royal Crown Three-Cushion Billiards Tournament. The result of my performance in the contest is, of course, inconsequential to our adventure, but I did reach the quarter-finals, during which round, I am disappointed to say, I was soundly defeated. Yet I can rest assured that I rank among the eight most proficient billiards-players in England.

"After having viewed the final round—in which one of the competitors made an astounding run of seventeen successive billiards—I decided to take a late supper and brandy at a local restaurant. I struck up a conversation with a gentleman—Philip Cheswycke, by name—sitting alone at a table adjacent to mine. Following our introductions, Cheswycke mentioned that he had heard of my recently-published *Lost World*, and was fascinated by the prehistoric themes presented in the novel. I thanked him for his kind words and continued the conversation by asking what his particular interest in antiquities might be. He responded that his fascination was not with antiquities *per se*, but with the fact that I had correctly placed humans and dinosaurs as having been contemporaneous. He heartily congratulated me on the accuracy of my depiction and said, without solicitation from me, that he was appalled by what he labelled as 'the Piltdown scourge' he had read about in the newspapers.

" 'It is impossible for such a "man" to have existed', he insisted, 'for it would contradict every logical sensibility as well as the doctrine of Biblical truth.'

" 'Well, sir', I responded, 'there *are* those who think that there may be other possible explanations for the source of humankind. Perhaps another equally feasible explanation could be that today's humans are the consequence of Darwinian descent. Given that, the Piltdown Man may well have been the anthropological prototype for modern mankind.'

"His body visibly trembled when I uttered those words, and he said: '*Impossible*! My good man, the Scriptures not only contain but *are* the words of God! Hence, all of their elements and all of their affirmations are absolutely errorless, and bind the faith and obedience of men. All of the affirmations of Scripture of all kinds, whether of spiritual doctrine or duty, of physical or historical fact, of psychological or philosophical principle, are *without any error.*'

"The vigour with which he made his statement threw me aback momentarily, but I quickly recovered when I realised that I might be in the presence of a *bona fide* Evangelical, so I continued the conversation.

"I said, 'Please, Mr Cheswycke, be so kind as to refrain from assuming my association with or acceptance of Darwinian theory. What I am asking, however, is this: Is

not your ascription of the origin of humankind similar to
that assumed by those Christians who believe in the literal
inerrancy of the Bible? They are called "Evangelicals", I
believe.'

" 'You are indeed correct, Dr Doyle. I—that is, the
group with which I am associated—have embarked on a
crusade to preserve the Truth and, by so doing, safeguard
the Christian ideals that will lead us from the tribulations
and trivialities of worldly existence to the sanctity of the
Kingdom of Heaven. And you, sir; what is your position
on this matter?'

"At this point, Charles, I perceived an opening. My
tactic was to comprehend as best I could the underlying
philosophy and strategy of the Evangelicals; so I indulged
my new-found friend.

" 'Frankly, Mr Cheswycke, I, too, am not so enamoured of the Modernist movement, and have been searching for a vehicle for venting my disapproval in a
constructive way. Perhaps you can assist me in this by
introducing me to your fellow-believers, for which I
would be grateful.'

" 'By all means, Dr Doyle', my friend responded, in a
voice that betrayed what I perceived as excited interest in
increasing the membership of his organisation."

Doyle continued his story: "We finished our supper,
and left the restaurant. Following Cheswycke's instructions, I drove with him in my motor to Ilford, a small
town in Essex about six miles south-east of London. We

arrived at a delapidated building lit only by lamps on the inside. Apart from the dull glow that shone through the curtained windows, there was no other light to be seen in any direction. Two unoccupied carriages, each harnessed to a horse feeding from an oat-bag, waited outside. I was shown in by Cheswycke, who did not announce himself before he entered.

"The front door led into a room which could not have measured any more than nine feet to a side. There was a door leading into another room, which was not illuminated. The walls were lined with shelves of books, none of whose titles I could discern because of the poor lighting. A small square table sat upon a dark-coloured carpet in the middle of the room. There were four chairs placed around the table, two of which were occupied by the men to whom I would presently be introduced.

" 'My brothers, I would like to introduce Arthur Conan Doyle, the creator of Sherlock Holmes', were Cheswycke's first words. The men looked up at me, and I down at them, for they did not get up from their seats.

" 'I am Barton Thackery,' said the one; 'I am Jonathan Preston', said the other. Neither offered to shake my hand.

"I could not help but notice that Preston had a symbol pinned to the lapel of his coat. It was a cross of the same design and aspect as the one on the notes that were sent to you and Teilhard."

"You mean you found the parties responsible for the threats?"
I asked with eager anticipation.

"Not necessarily, Charles", Doyle responded. "There
could be hundreds—perhaps thousands—of men sporting the same medallion. You may remember that you
told me that the letters and indeed the package of relics
you received were post-marked 'London'. That does not
necessarily mean that they *originated* in London. They
could have been prepared anywhere within a fifty-mile
radius and somehow transferred to London, where they
were post-marked and forwarded for delivery to you and
Teilhard."

"Yes, yes, of course", I said. "Please continue."

"We struck up a conversation about how moderate
elements were challenging Christian orthodoxy. I must
admit it was at times difficult for me to agree convincingly
with the positions of the three men in the room, but I
feel confident that I was successful since they seemed to
speak freely about their attitudes to what they described
as 'the pestilence of Modernist apostasy'.

"These Christians feel much more strongly about their
beliefs than I had imagined, Charles. I am convinced that
Evangelicalism insists on doctrinal conformity, enforced
by an authoritarian leadership and reinforced by spiritual
coercion that threatens the *pain of Hell*—their very
words—for any who dare to depart from the dogmatic
prescription. They told me that they would stop at

nothing to free the world of Godlessness. 'The heretical Modernist community', said an animated Preston at one point, 'would be well advised to take good care, for in Jesus' own words in Matthew 24:22, . . . *there should be no flesh saved: but for the elect's sake THOSE DAYS SHALL BE SHORTENED.* We shall abide by the words of our Lord.'

"I felt a sense of threat by that utterance and, not wanting to overstay my welcome after having listened to them for almost an hour, I bade gratitude for their time and begged my leave. Before I departed, however, I asked if they knew of an arm of their organisation that is situated in or near the Crowborough/Uckfield area. Cheswycke said that he did, and gave to me its locality."

"And where might it be?" I asked Doyle.

"On the Barkham farm."

At eight o'clock in the evening on Wednesday, 18 December 1912, Aubrey Strahan[70] called the Burlington House meeting of the Royal Geological Society to order. The chamber was packed. This meeting, I would learn later, was to be the best attended in the history of the Society. The agenda indicated that I would speak first about the geology of the area of the Piltdown find, to

---

[70] Strahan (1852–1928), a geologist, was president of the Society from 1912 to 1914.

be followed by Smith Woodward's presentation, during which he would unveil his reconstruction for the world to see and address the evolutionary significance of Sussex Man. Finally, Grafton Elliot Smith[71] was to discuss the importance of the features of the neuro-cranial endocast.[72]

I began my exposition by unveiling the remains. There was applause from the audience as soon as I removed the linen cloth covering them. Then, using a series of lantern-slides to assist me in explaining the geology of the Weal-den area, I mentioned that the artifacts were recovered from flint-bearing gravel-deposits in the central Weald which, I pointed out, had neither been mapped nor recorded before. I then indicated that it was appropriate to assume that the bones were contemporaneous with the gravels— specifically, Lower Pleistocene. The other animal remains, I said, were most likely somewhat older. Finally, I indicated that "whether artificial or natural, many of the eoliths closely resemble those found in the High Plateau gravels at Igtham."

The comments and criticisms of my presentation were varied but not unfriendly. The discussion centred on which of the relics belonged to the Pliocene and/or Pleistocene epochs. A sampling of opinion follows.

---

[71] Smith (1871–1937) was a neuroanatomist and anthropologist. He was knighted in 1934.
[72] A cast of the inner surface of the cranium which allows study of the convolutions of the brain.

Sollas[73]: I regard the deposits which were laid down during the Pleistocene period as forming, when superimposed, a thickness or depth of 4,000 feet. I estimate that the formation has proceeded at the rate of a foot per century, and that therefore the collective deposits of the Pleistocene period probably have taken about four hundred thousand years to form.

Rutot[74]: My estimate is an age of one hundred and forty thousand years, as founded on a prolonged study of the Pleistocene formations found along the river valleys of Belgium.

Penck[75]: After studying the changes produced by Alpine glaciers during the Pleistocene cycles of extreme cold, I am of the opinion that such changes indicate for the Pleistocene period a duration of at least half a million years. The glaciers may have been occupied as much as a million and a half years. These figures are, however, provisional estimates, subject to modification as our knowledge increases. The numerous changes in climate, of elevation and depression in the land, the transformation of our animals, the elaboration of human culture, the evolution and distribution of human races, all bespeak an enormously long period of time.

---

[73] William Johnson Sollas (1849–1936), Oxford University professor of geology.
[74] A. Louis Rutot (1847–1933), Belgian geologist.
[75] Albrecht Penck (1858–1945), German geologist.

Dawkins: I agree with the authors of the paper that the deposit containing the human remains belonged to the Pleistocene age, and that the Pliocene mammalia in it— *Mastodon arvernensis* and the rest—had been derived from a Pliocene stratum formerly existing in that area. Man is an evolutionary product of the Pleistocene, and first reached Britain about the middle of that epoch.

Moir: It was impossible to speak with confidence, but the whole evidence suggested that the Piltdown deposit and the plateau on which it rests are not preglacial or even early Pleistocene; they belong to a period long after the first cold period had passed away, but they occur at the very base of the great implement-bearing succession of Paleolithic deposits in the south-east of England.

Kennard[76]: The Galley Hill man must have been almost contemporaneous with the very primitive human being reconstructed by Dr Smith Woodward.

Newton[77]: The highly mineralised condition of the

---

[76] Alfred Santer Kennard (1870–1948), London businessman and amateur paleontologist. The so-called Galley Hill Man was discovered in 200,000-year-old gravels high on the Thames terrace south of London in 1888. The skeletal remains, which were of modern aspect, were found along with primitive stone tools, making their owner the most archaic "modern" human yet discovered. The British scientific community was elated to tell the world that there were humans looking exactly like us walking around in England more than 2,000 centuries in the past. Unfortunately, their elation would not last very long, for on the sixtieth anniversary of the find it was shown by fluorine dating that the Galley Hill specimen was in truth only about 3,200 years old. Arthur Keith was among the most ardent supporters of the authenticity of the remains.
[77] Edwin Tulley Newton (1840–1930), paleontologist who first described Galley Hill finds to the Society in 1896.

specimens seemed to point to their being of Pliocene age rather than Pleistocene.

Abbott[78]: Having given much time to master the later geological history of the Weald, it is my opinion that two ages are represented in the Piltdown gravels. The lower or bottom stratum, which contained the Pliocene remains and human bones, is Pliocene in date; the upper levels, in which the rude Paleolithic implements lay, had been disturbed at a later time, and are to be regarded as Pleistocene in age.

Keith: I am pursuaded that Mr Dawson and Dr Smith Woodward were ultra-cautious in assigning a Pleistocene date to the human remains found at Piltdown. All the evidence seems to point to a Pliocene age. Hence the importance of their discovery, for although the handiwork of Pliocene man has been recognised for a considerable number of years, the man himself was unknown until Mr Dawson brought him into the light of day.

I thanked the members of the Society for their active interest and participation in my presentation and summed up thus: "I am quite prepared, from an anthropological point of view, to accept an earlier date for the origin of the human remains, and Dr Smith Woodward and I had

---

[78] William James Lewis Abbott (1863–1933), London jeweler and amateur geologist.

perhaps erred on the side of caution in placing the date as early Pleistocene. It is possible that the Piltdown race may belong to a period preceding the Pleistocene, that is, the Pliocene." I then relinquished the floor.

Smith Woodward followed me by describing to the assembled membership each of the nine cranial fragments and the mandible. After explaining how and why he believed they belonged to the same individual, he removed the cloth shroud from his reconstruction. There was lengthy applause. "The cranial fragments", he said, "were sufficiently well-preserved to exhibit the shape and natural relations of the frontal, parietal, occipital and temporal bones, and to justify the reconstruction of some other elements [namely, the jaw] by inference." Then, Smith Woodward explained his reasons for the relationship between the cranial remains and the jaw fragment: they were found close to the skull, and they were similar in colouration and condition.

"I propose that the Piltdown specimen be regarded as a new genus of the family Hominidae, to be named *Eoanthropus* ["Dawn Man"]", he said solemnly. "The species to which the skull and mandible have now been described in detail may be named *Eoanthropus dawsoni*, in honour of its discoverer."

As I stood to acknowledge the thunderous applause of the membership, I said to myself: "Dawson, old chap, you did it. *You did it!*"

The sweetest dessert of all, however, was served up by Smith Woodward flashing upon the lantern-screen the following diagram:

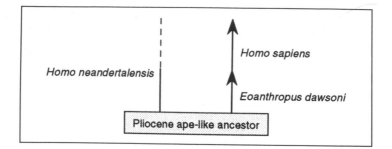

The fraudulent remains had been accepted by one of the world's leading paleo-anthropologists as intermediate to apes and humans and, more significantly, as *a direct linear ancestor of modern Man.*[79]

---

[79]The following day, *The New York Times* reported on the meeting:

MAN HAD REASON BEFORE HE SPOKE

Most Remarkable of the Discoveries
Due to the Finding of the Piltdown Skull.

IS A REAL MISSING LINK

Anything Earlier, if Found, Will Prove to be Almost Entirely Ape,
Says Dr. Woodward—Scientists Excited.

By Marconi Transatlantic Wireless Telegraph to The New York Times

LONDON, Dec. 19.—Extraordinary interest has been aroused among anthropologists by Dr. A.S. Woodward's paper on the Piltdown skull read at a meeting of the Geological Society yesterday. No other event in the annals of the society has created such a profound sensation among the members.

But there was more to the pudding. Following Smith Woodward, Grafton Elliot Smith summed up his own presentation by saying to the audience: "The Sussex specimen has the most primitive and most simian brain so far recorded; one, moreover, *such as might reasonably have been expected to be associated in one and the same individual with*

In some quarters it is even believed that the skull, from certain apelike characteristics, may prove the existence of the "missing link," or the most important of several missing links, in the chain of the evolution of man.

"That this skull, representing a hitherto unknown human species, is the missing link I, for one, have not the slightest doubt," said Dr. Woodward to an interviewer. "This discovery takes us back nearer to the source and origin of the first living creature than any other discovery ever made.

"Hitherto the nearest approach to a species from which we might have been said to descend that had been discovered was the cave-man, but the authorities constantly asserted that we did not spring direct from the cave-man. Where, then, was the missing link in the chain of our evolution?

"To me, at any rate, the answer lies in the Piltdown skull, for we came direct from a species almost entirely ape.

"Of course, there may be more missing links, but if we are to find them we shall have to discover human remains of greater antiquity than those brought to light at Piltdown. Such a discovery, to my mind, would bring us to almost pure ape.

"The most significant thing about the discovery does not so much lie in the fact that the brain is infinitely smaller than that of an ordinary human being, or that the jaw is a jaw of a chimpanzee, but in the fact, proved beyond any doubt from the shape of the jaw, that the creature when alive did not possess the power of speech.

"But that it had some brain is certain. Therefore in the evolution of the human species the brain came first and speech was the growth of a later age."

Dr. Woodward seems to be of the opinion that the possessor of the skull did not exceed 5 feet in height, and further that, owing to the slight development of the brow ridges and the slenderness of the jaw, it may the the skull of a female.

the mandible which so definitely indicates the zoölogical rank of its original possessor."

I could barely contain my delight with the results.

The general discussion that followed the formal presentations made it obvious that not everyone assembled would accept Smith Woodward's interpretation of the Piltdown remains. The discussants divided along two lines of enquiry: the age of the fossils, and whether or not the cranial fragments and the mandible had belonged to the same creature. There were two factions within each group. There were some who believed that the remains were of Pliocene origin and others who felt they were Pleistocene. And there were members who agreed with Smith Woodward that the skull and jaw belonged together; but there were some who did not.

Of the nine participants in the discussion following Smith Woodward's presentation, two of them (Dawkins and Duckworth)[80] took the monistic position, that is, all of the fragments—including the mandible—had belonged to a single being. Waterston[81] was the only speaker who reserved opinion on both counts: he would postulate neither the age of the remains nor whether or not they were of the same animal.

---

[80] Wynfrid Laurence Henry Duckworth (1870–1956) was an anatomist and physical anthropologist.
[81] David Waterston (1871–1942) was an anatomist. His criticism of the Piltdown remains was anathema to Smith Woodward.

I followed the debate with rapt attention, and witnessed the thrusts and parries as if I were attending a fencing match. I had accomplished precisely what I set out to do: introduce bogus fossils to the scientific community, have them accepted as authentic, and fuel an empty and worthless controversy over meaningless artifacts. "What fools these scientists are", I thought. *"What bloody fools!"*

And the debate continued in trumps during the weeks and months following the Society meeting. The most vociferous detractor of Smith Woodward's theorising and reconstruction was Arthur Keith. He had purchased a complete set of casts that was produced by the Damon Company in Weymouth. The collection included all of the bone fragments, the endo-cranial cast made by Grafton Elliot Smith, Smith Woodward's reconstructed skull, and the eoliths and paleoliths.

Keith saw blatant errors in Smith Woodward's skull. The jaw and the cranium, he suggested, were rather too ape-like. Smith Woodward, Keith felt, had somewhat unsuccessfully tried to reconcile a modern human brain-case with a primitive jaw. The brain-case, in fact, had been reconstructed with a total misunderstanding of cranial anatomy. To give the appearance of modernity, Keith said, Smith Woodward had reconstructed the skull to reflect the asymmetry of human skulls (the left and right sides are not equal in size due to lobal specialisation related to the ability to speak). Keith's position was that the brain should be more symmetrical and, so too, should the brain-case.

Keith argued his case: "The height of the brain-chamber should be increased by almost a centimetre and one-third. The width and fullness should be enlarged. The brain capacity should be augmented; the shape of the brain should be changed. The anomalous configurations of the occipital bone and the extreme asymmetry of the lamboidal suture[82] should almost disappear, and all the points we are familiar with in human skulls should leap to the eye."

Keith noted the modern aspect of the glenoid fossa[83] and of the molar teeth. This, he said, argues against the "chimpanzoid" mandible presented by Smith Woodward and in favour of the missing symphysis housing modern, but large, teeth.

With these conclusions in mind, Keith defiantly (perhaps the result of an arrogant pride?)—but confidently—requested a dentist friend of his, J. Leon Williams, to reconstruct the jaw according to these revised specifications.

The consequences of the Keith–Smith Woodward *tête-à-tête* were no less than fascinating. A comparison of the two reconstructions will distinctly illustrate the difference in morphological interpretation between the two men. Smith Woodward's reconstruction of the Piltdown skull is shown in the photograph opposite.

The viewer will notice four significant elements of this

---

[82] The lamboidal suture is the line along which the occipital and parietal bones are joined.
[83] The depression in the skull that receives the mandibular condyle.

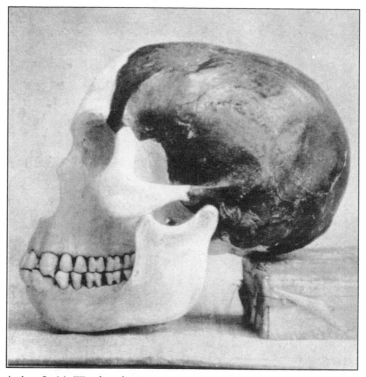

Arthur Smith Woodward's reconstruction of the Piltdown skull features a small brain capacity and an ape-like jaw.

reconstruction: (1) the jaw is prognathous, that is, it juts out as in an ape; (2) there is no chin; (3) the cranial capacity is somewhat smallish—it is only about 1,070 cubic centimetres; and (4) the canines are large relative to the other teeth. On balance, Smith Woodward's reconstruction reflects a human-like cranium coupled to an ape-like jaw (including the flattened molar teeth).

A view of the top of the skull shows how Smith Woodward assembled the cranial fragments to achieve a brain capacity of slightly more than 1,000 cubic centimetres:

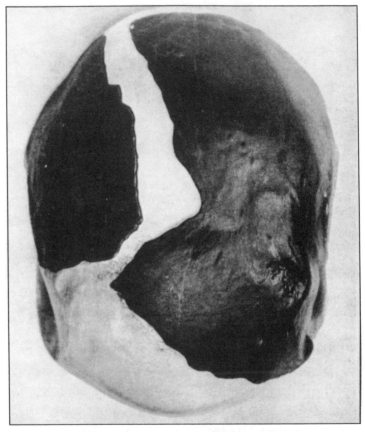

Smith Woodward's cranial reconstruction as seen from above. An erroneous placement of the great blood channel by nearly a full inch from its proper position results in a skull capacity of 1,070cc. It can also be seen that the two sides of the skull are rather close together.

Arthur Keith's reconstruction of the remains indicates the depth to which the controversy would run:

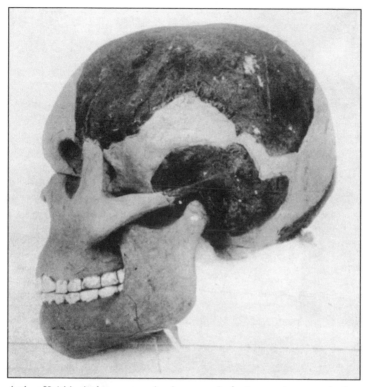

Arthur Keith's rival reconstruction increases the brain capacity to nearly that of modern man. The jaw, too, is of a more modern aspect.

It can be seen in Keith's assembly that the jaw is rendered less prognathous and that the canines are smaller and flatter. The cranial capacity has also been increased by about 400 cubic centimetres.

A bird's-eye view of Keith's cranial reconstruction is shown below:

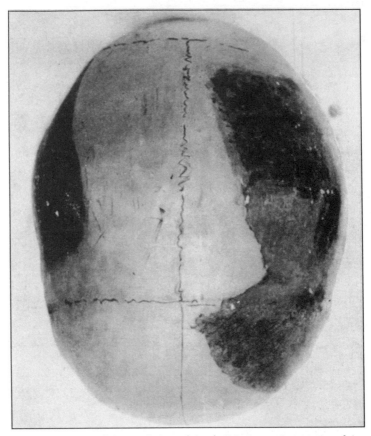

Keith's separation of the two halves of the skull increases the capacity of the Piltdown skull to 1,500cc, "a really large brain [even] for a modern man," according to him. It was Keith's interpretation of the cranial and mandibular remains that set the stage for the rivalry that would ultimately lead to the end of his long personal relationship with Smith Woodward.

Keith's rival reconstruction was, I am convinced, at least partially the result of his sense of insult over not being invited by Smith Woodward to study the remains immediately. The controversy between Keith and Smith Woodward had, I must say with some satisfaction, become quite heated at times.

Keith first showed his version of the Piltdown skull to Grafton Elliot Smith, who was shocked when he saw it. In response to his incredulity, Smith wrote to Smith Woodward that he (Smith) was "quite convinced that we shall have to modify [Smith Woodward's] restoration in some respects".

Smith Woodward was finally able to view Keith's reconstruction at the Royal College of Surgeons on 10 July 1913. He requested that I accompany him, and I accepted. To rouse the storm a bit, I suggested to Smith Woodward during our cab ride that Keith had perhaps arranged the skull-bones and mandible in an effort to have them suit his own personal human evolutionary interpretations. Smith Woodward commented to me that the rival reconstruction would most likely turn out to be "an amusing heresy".

The competition between the two contenders had reached a stage where, on one occasion, Keith said—with what was described by a witness as "infinite scorn"—that "the creature represented by Smith Woodward's reconstruction could neither eat nor, for that matter, even breathe!" "Every evidence", Keith continued, "contradicts the mandible's possession of a large canine. *It could not have held an ape-like eye-tooth.*"

At their confrontation at the Royal College of Surgeons, Keith said to Smith Woodward in an obviously belligerent tone, "But, alas, Arthur, in the last analysis you cannot at all defend your reconstruction, for there is no eye-tooth available", to which Smith Woodward responded, "Yes, that is true at the moment. However, when it *is* found, I can assure you it would look like a chimpanzee's but the wear patterns would be human-like. The canine will project slightly above the molars, be much larger than that in modern Man, and be separated from the next rear-most tooth by a diastema to allow meshing with the upper canine. Only the missing canine itself will provide irrefutable evidence of the mandible's possessor."

"Then we must have the eye-tooth", responded Keith. "And, I assure you, my friend, that when it is found, it will without any doubt whatsoever vindicate my reconstruction—and more appropriately than it would under any circumstance suit yours."

It was very clear that the contest between the two Arthurs had reached the point of pitched battle. Not only was each of their professional reputations on the line, but there was the new spice of personal strife. This was not to be the end of the controversy; it would expand during the months to come. It was similarly very clear how invaluable the discovery of the missing canine would be towards settling the issue once and for all.

At that point, my face flushed and, with what may have been an almost audible gasp, I suddenly remembered that *I still had the original canine*, safely contained in the mandibular symphysis that Teilhard and I had dissociated from the body of the jaw!

I next saw Teilhard—at long last—on a Saturday morning, 30 August 1913. He had just finished a period of retreat at Ore Place following a trip to the Continent to visit his family and attend to other business. He visited me at my home early enough for us to breakfast together, during which time I filled him in on the details.

"The meeting of the Society in December last was a particular success", I said. "The controversy between Keith and Smith Woodward is simmering beautifully."

"Yes, I understand that it is", Teilhard commented. "I have been following the story in *Le Monde* and *Nature*. The reconstruction of the skull seems to be the issue on which the battle was joined, and it appears that only discovery of the canine will settle it."

"Right you are, old friend. And your arrival here this morning is truly serendipitous, for I am expecting to meet none other than Arthur Smith Woodward today, and we shall be visiting the gravel-pit. We have been visiting the site on a regular basis since June, with no success, of course."

"And the canine?" Teilhard asked.

I smiled. "You remember that we agreed to save the teeth contained in the mandibular symphysis, do you not? I extracted the canine after realising during the July meeting of the College of Surgeons how important it would be. In view of the members' debate concerning the eye-tooth's expected appearance, I spent many a day and night designing on paper a tooth that would be attractive to both Keith's and Smith Woodward's expectations. It is now sculpted, stained, and ready to be found."

"May I see it?"[84]

Teilhard and I drove over by carriage to meet Smith Woodward at the station. After greeting each other warmly, Teilhard enthusiastically congratulated Smith Woodward on his presentation of 18th December at the Society. We then drove immediately to the Barkham farm and walked to the gravel-pit where we were met by that

---

[84] The following illustration shows the results of Dawson's artistry:

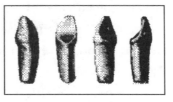

The drawing was printed as part of "Supplementary note on the discovery of a Palaeolithic human skull and mandible at Piltdown (Sussex)," *Quarterly Journal of the Geological Society* 70 (April 1914).

infernally pesky goose, Chipper. He was indeed a nasty brute, and would not leave us alone. Geese, as I understand it, can be particularly territorial. At one point of extreme annoyance, Teilhard looked up at me and with feigned innocence asked: "Charles, have you ever tasted roast goose?"

The day was hot and Teilhard, poor man, was dressed completely in black. He was perspiring profusely as we three went digging and rummaging through the pit. We searched in vain for quite a while. Then—finally— Teilhard shouted: "Yes. Yes! *I think I have found the canine! Charles! Arthur! I HAVE THE CANINE!*"

Smith Woodward could not immediately believe that Teilhard had hit pay-dirt since throughout the day we had been finding small pieces of iron-stone that resembled in shape a canine tooth. However, after a few minutes of inspection, Smith Woodward verified that "Yes, indeed!" Teilhard had found the one and only piece of evidence that could vindicate his reconstruction of the Piltdown skull. Smith Woodward was beside himself with joy and satisfaction.

I caught a glance at Teilhard, who winked at me.

An invitation to stay for dinner was begged off by Smith Woodward, who said he was returning immediately to London to see how the tooth would fit into its reconstructed mandibular socket.

"*Perfectly*", I said to myself, as we climbed into my carriage. "*It would fit perfectly.*"

* * *

On 16 September 1913 Smith Woodward triumphantly
announced the discovery of the canine tooth to the British
Association for the Advancement of Science at Central
Hall in Birmingham. In what seemed like a reprise of the
Geological Society meeting the previous December, the
news was leaked to the *Daily Express* (unbeknownst to
me, it appeared in print in the 2nd September issue). I
must admit that I was rather upset at the leak, and said
in confidence to Smith Woodward: "The worst is that I
have no doubt it was done by someone who ought to
have known better. It is a great pity and undermines
things in more ways than one, and I am very annoyed
by it."

The BAAS meeting turned out to be the sparring
match that I had expected to take place between Smith
Woodward and Keith. In his presentation, Smith Woodward stated that the eye-tooth proves beyond doubt that
the Piltdown Man had ape-like dentition. The teeth were
not, he stressed, similar to those of humans, as Keith had
suggested.

With the tooth now revealed, Keith retreated somewhat from his heretofore intransigent position. He said
that the roots of the tooth do, in fact, appear to be human.
However, he insisted, the volume of the Sussex specimen's
brain must still definitely be as large as a modern human's. He also persisted in emphasising his belief that

the left and right sides of the brain were of similar size (a primitive characteristic), the reason being that ancestral creatures—which have no preference for left- or right-handedness and which have no ability to speak—would not have developed asymmetrical brains.

Yet Smith Woodward continued to maintain that it was his interpretation that was correct. The left side of the brain should be larger than the right because the Piltdown Man was of recent enough vintage to have developed the ability to speak, and his brain specialised in response to that aptitude. (It was now believed by a large segment of the scientific community that the remains were of the order of 500,000 years old.)

The meeting ended in a stand-off. Both Smith Woodward and Keith held tenaciously to their contentions, neither budging so much as an intellectual inch.

Presently, the fireworks would commence in earnest. Grafton Elliot Smith wrote a letter to *Nature* (published 2 October 1913) which suggested that Keith's misinterpretation of the remains might be attributable to his not having had access to the original material. This letter turned out to exacerbate the situation further. Smith wrote another letter (*Nature*, 13 November 1913) in which he said that he had, in fact, seen the original, and that Keith's reconstruction was wrong. Keith exploded in a tantrum upon reading this.

The debate continued well into the following year,

with Keith insisting that his restoration of the remains was correct, and Smith persisting that it was in error.

Finally, Keith took it upon himself to reassemble a skull that had been separated into pieces by an independent party. Incredibly, his reconstruction turned out to be accurate to within 20 cubic centimetres.[85]

The controversy would not die.

Nor would my concern about the threats made against both Teilhard and myself. The fear of a violent end never

---

[85] Keith himself described the exercise in his book, *The Antiquity of Man*, 2 vols. (London: Williams & Norgate, 1915), under a chapter heading called "An Experiment in Reconstruction":

The question is often asked: Are four fragments of a skull sufficient to give us a definite clue to the original form of the skull? Apparently not; at least it was clear that reconstructions by Dr Smith Woodward and by myself indicated men of a totally different type. To test the matter, Professor F. G. Parsons of St Thomas's Hospital Medical School, London, made a proposal to me, namely, that he and some of his fellow-anatomists should select a skull, cut fragments from it corresponding to those found at Piltdown, and that I should attempt to reconstruct the entire skull from these fragments. I gladly accepted the proposal, and resolved, however the results should turn out, to make the experiment the subject of an address I had promised to the fellows of the Royal Anthropological Institute.

On January 16th, 1914, a fortnight before my lecture was due, the four pieces of a skull . . . came to me from Dr Douglas Derry of University College, London. They were the representatives of the Piltdown fragments, and the task of reconstruction offered the same difficulties. Only on one piece—the occipital fragment—could any certain sign of the middle line of the skull be detected.

. . . The actual reconstruction of the experimental skull occupied me the better part of two days. . . . [Dr Derry] then showed me the cast of the original—the skull of an ancient Egyptian—a woman, with a peculiar form of head and a brain capacity of 1395 c.c. The estimate I returned of the escaped my mind. It pervaded my every act and thought. I wondered what the "Barkham farm" connexion that Doyle had alluded to meant. As far as I knew, there were only four persons directly associated with the estate: the chief tenant at the Manor, Robert Kenward, and his twenty-seven-year-old daughter, Mabel;[86] George Maryon-Wilson, the owner of the property; and Venus Hargreaves, a day-labourer who tended to a variety of duties on the farm. Hargreaves, who lived and worked in what at one time served as an oast-house, had also on occasion helped me with shovelling earth from the pit. I had never seen or heard of any other persons in regular attendance.

I was soon to make Doyle aware of this cast of characters, for he requested a rather hastily-appointed 10th November visit with me. We conversed over lunch at the pub.

After our whiskys had arrived, Doyle removed his note-case from his coat pocket and dislodged from it a folded newspaper clipping. He opened it and handed it to me.

It was from the 8th November issue of the *Ilford Sun-Chronicle*. I was taken by almost uncontrollable horror when I read it.

---

brain capacity, namely, 1415 c.c., was not very wide of the truth . . . I was relieved to find [that I had constructed] a fairly accurate reproduction of the original.

[86] Mabel Kenward, who was born in 1885, was twenty-seven years old in 1912.

Ilford Resident Found Murdered!

Respected businessman's tongue is severed

Left to die with dagger in his heart

Town's residents are appalled

Police have no clue to identity of killer.

ILFORD, 7 November:—Mr Philip Cheswycke, a respected resident and successful accountant in Ilford, has been found dead in the Northwoods area. His body was discovered by two youths who were hunting rabbits.

The respected businessman was found with a dagger imbedded in his heart and his tongue cut out. The tongue, which lay upon his chest, had a small object thrust into it in the shape of a cross.

Police are at a loss as to who the murderer is; nor have they any motive for the act. [etc., etc.]

"My word, Conan!" I said quietly. "They can and will commit murder!" And then my mouth went dry: "They know who you are, Conan. They know your name! *They know your bloody name!*"

"Yes, Charles, they do. But we also know theirs. And you may also remember", Doyle continued, "that I have friends—well, admirers, at least—in Scotland Yard. I shall speak with them tomorrow."

"No, Conan, you cannot go to the police! If you do they will ask questions, and those questions will lead to other questions which will lead to our hoax being exposed. Speaking to the police is out of the question."

"You are willing to risk your life for your charade?"

"I have no choice, Conan. My reputation is at stake. I would not be able to live the rest of my life in humiliation. I must take the chance. However", I continued, "if you feel you must speak with the police, then follow the dictates of your conscience. I cannot force silence upon you."

"Not on your life, Charles. Sorry about the awkward phrasing, old chap, but we pledged along with Teilhard that we would be in this together to the end. I shall stick to my pledge. In that regard, should Teilhard be informed of this latest development?"

"I think not, Conan. There is nothing gained in worsening his already-endangered life. Let us agree not to tell him."

"Fine", said Doyle.

"But what of the reference made by Cheswycke to the Barkham farm?" I asked.

"We must speak to each of the four persons associated with the estate," Doyle responded. "I am convinced that one of them has a direct connexion to the Evangelicals I met in Ilford. Who amongst the four might be available to interview now?"

"I do not know for sure, but I imagine that Hargreaves must be somewhere on the property since he works there all day."

"Then let us get into my motor and go."

We downed the last of our ale and set off towards Piltdown.

We spotted Hargreaves as we were driving up the road to Barkham Manor. He was making repairs to the entrance-gate.

"Afternoon, gents", he said as we approached. "How are you keeping this fine day?"

"Good-day, Hargreaves", I said. "I'm fine, thank you. I think you may have already made the acquaintance of my friend, Conan Doyle."

"Aye, sir, I have. Good to see you again, Dr Doyle."

"Good to see you, too, Hargreaves."

"Hargreaves, if you have a few minutes, we should like to speak with you and ask a few questions", I said.

"Righty-ho. No problem at all. I could do with a sit back anyways. Been working since six this morning. Me quarters are just over there. Come on in for a cuppa."

When we arrived at his residence, he suggested that he should "do us a fresh brew-up, since this here tea's been sitting since this morning".

"Thank you", I said, "but it really is not necessary."

"Then . . . um . . . if you both promise to keep it quiet, we can have some of *this* if you like", said Hargreaves in a whisper as he dislodged a hip-flask from his pocket.

"Oh, no thank you, Hargreaves", said Doyle with a

gracious smile as he waved the flask away. "On second thoughts, I think we would prefer some tea, if that is no trouble."

"Not at all", was the response, as Hargreaves carefully returned the flask to his trousers. "Now, gentlemen, what can I do for you?"

Our questioning began amid a clamour of pots and pans and rather rude handling of dishes. With all of the indelicacy Hargreaves afforded his china, I was amazed that any remained with which to serve us. I said to myself that this man could be neither a conspirator nor a murderer.

"Hargreaves, are you aware of any guests—strangers—having visited the estate recently, say, within the past two or three months?" Doyle asked.

"Visitors? Hmm, let me think. I don't know for certain . . . but . . . Aye! We did have some visitors, oh, 'bout three, mebbe four weeks ago."

"Do you know how many there were?"

"Well, I think there were six, mebbe eight. They met in the Manor reception-hall. They were here for some sort of meeting. It were a right grand affair, with help hired just to deal with the cooking and serving and such like."

"Mm, I see. And can you describe any of the guests for me?"

"Lumme, they were a fine-looking lot! They all drove up in their own carriages, all got up like a dog's dinner . . ."

I stifled a smile.

"Did you get to meet and speak with any of them?" asked Doyle.

"Not really, but they seemed nice enough. One of them even give me an odd sort of gift as he was leaving. It's around here somewhere; I put it away being as I couldn't quite make out the use of it. Now where would it have got to?"

A cacophony of clanging and banging again reverberated throughout the room as Hargreaves searched his belongings. The din finally ceased with "Hullo! Here it is!"

Hargreaves showed Doyle and me a small cross mounted as a lapel pin.

"Do you remember the name of the person who gave this to you?" I asked.

"Hmm . . . let me see. I'm not sure, but it was something like Hacker or Packer or something like that."

"Thackery, perhaps?" I suggested.

"Aye, Mr Dawson, it was Thackery. A fine gent. Spoke real nice to me. Even asked fer God's blessing on me afore he left. Fancy, he even asked *me* to the Manor when he returns here."

"And when might that be?" Doyle wondered.

"Coming up on the twenty-eighth—this Sunday, sir. Two in the afternoon. Mr Kenward is paying me an extra quid to set up loads of benches in the morning on account of there's another meeting laid on, with a whole mob of people coming from all over. The gov'nor thinks it'll be all right for me to nip in for a listen."

"Thank you, Hargreaves", said Doyle abruptly. "You have been very helpful. No need to show us out. We know the way. Thanks again and good-day to you."

"Aye. But hold on! You both ought to come to the meeting. Mr Thackery said I should invite all me friends, and since you two gents is me friends I'm inviting you."

"Thank you, Hargreaves", I said.

As we walked back to Doyle's motor, he said solemnly, "Our attendance here on Sunday next will, I am sure, be of utmost interest and importance."

We arrived at Barkham Manor's reception-hall at exactly two in the afternoon. There was what seemed to me like a herd of horses in the field, each hitched to a carriage. The horses were in various states of consciousness. Some were quietly munching from an oat-bag; others were nibbling the grass at their feet; still others were sleeping in a one-rearhoof-cocked position. However the *pièce-de-résistance*, the *ne plus ultra* of transportation, sat outside the Manor entrance. Someone had arrived in a gleaming, black Rolls-Royce motor. Someone inside was very well-off indeed.

Upon entering, Doyle and I saw that the room was filled to over-capacity, forcing us to be among the many standees. There must have been well over three hundred

people in attendance. The front of the room was graced
with a lectern surrounded by flowers of all types and
colours. To the left of the lectern was a grand piano at
which was seated a matronly woman. There were hand-
painted signs posted on the walls throughout the room:
"ALCOHOL IS THE DEVIL'S POTION", "EVOLUTION IS SA-
TAN'S WORK", "THE BIBLE IS THE LIVING WORD OF
GOD".

Presently, the music began. Three hundred voices sang
in unison the hymn "God's Home Eterne".

Will your short stay on Earth be deserving
For entrance to God's home eterne;
Or will you be welcomed by Satan—
A sinner in Hell's fire to burn?

After this musical preamble, none other than Barton
Thackery approached the lectern. The mood was trans-
formed into one of silent anticipation as he leisurely surveyed the mass of people. And then he spoke.

"All rise . . . Let us pray. *Heavenly Father, we beseech*
you to forgive us our sins. Teach us that only the true Christian
faith, based on the Word of God, is capable of producing a
conscientious, joyful, and vital Christian life. Teach us that
the true Christian, with his salvation based securely on the
Word of God, is sure of his salvation and, therefore, of eternal
life. Teach us to feed our souls each day on Your sacred Scrip-
tures, for only there will we daily discover new promise. Teach

us that the true Christian has a vision of the life beyond as brilliant and enrapturing because of its promised joy—eternal life in the presence of Jesus Christ. Teach us to follow the words of Jesus in John 12:26—'If any man serve me, let him follow me; and where I am, there shall also my servant be: if any man serve me, him will my Father honour.' Amen."

In chorus: "Amen."

"Please be seated. We are honoured today by the presence of a very special guest—the most renowned American minister of God's Word. He is devoting his life's work in service to Jesus Christ and to carrying our Lord's message to the masses. He has graciously agreed to join us today as part of his two-month tour of ministry. His next stop is London, where he will bring God's Word to perhaps a quarter of a million souls. Let us give a grand Sussex welcome to God's enemy of Satan, God's foe of sin, God's rival of alcohol, God's opponent of harlotry, God's messenger of the Gospel . . . God's soldier of Salvation. . . ."

Drum-roll on the piano's bass notes.

"Let us hail the conveyor of love, the rival of evolutionism, the adversary of Modernism, and the reigning apostle of Evangelicalism . . . William . . . Ashley . . . 'Billy' . . . *SUNDA-A-Y!*"

As Sunday walked towards the lectern, arms waving and face aglow amid the ear-shattering applause, the pianist played a rousing American tune called "Battle Hymn of the Republic"—written during the American Southern

Rebellion by Mrs Julia Ward Howe of Boston. Thackery began leading the congregation in song:

Mine eyes have seen the glory of the coming of the Lord;
He is trampling out the vintage where the grapes of wrath are stored;
He hath loosed the fateful lightning of His terrible swift sword;
His Truth is marching on!

Glory, glory, Hallejujah!
Glory, glory, Hallejujah!
Glory, glory, Hallejujah!
His Truth is marching on!

In the beauty of the lilies Christ was born across the sea,
With a glory in His bosom that transfigures you and me;
As he died to make men holy, let us die to make men free!
While God is marching on.

Glory, glory, Hallejujah!
Glory, glory, Hallejujah!
Glory, glory, Hallejujah!
While God is marching on!

Finally, the din subsided and Sunday took control.

"If you want to live in sin, all right, live in sin and go to Hell in the end!

The hour has come for plain speech. Everything the Devil's in favour of, I'm against. I'm against the theatre, because the Devil's in favour of it; I'm against booze and I'm against card-parties because the Devil's in favour of them. And dancing is a rotten, infernal, lustful, licentious practice."

The crowd was astonished.

"*I defy Unitarianism. I defy Christian Science, the worst folderol of the lot, the worst tommyrot that has ever come down the pike. I defy Hinduism and Shintoism and Zoroastrianism and Confucianism and Buddhism. I defy evolutionism—a theory of bastards, of Godless losers. The followers of such absurdities are all demented, silly, deluded fools, clouded by miserable, wistful philosophies dreamt up by shysters. They are all the devil's disciples. The devil loves them; the preacher does not.*"

By now, Sunday had begun to tighten his grip on the audience.

"*I curse biblical scholars, those anaemic, rank sceptics and their sneering, highbrow intellectualism. I know no more about theology than a jackrabbit does about table tennis or an elephant does about crocheting. Religion is not a study and a discourse; it is courage, deep faith and a test of will. I want to say that I believe the Bible is the Word of God from cover to cover. Not because I understand its philosophy, speculation or theory. I cannot; wouldn't attempt it; and I would be a fool if I tried. I believe in it because it is from the mouth of God.*

"*Evolutionists are shackling Christians with handcuffs of speculation and linking man to the rotting, vile, shrivelled, stenchful corpse of unbelief. They have unchained the passions of Hell. Any minister who believes and teaches evolution is a stinking skunk, a fraud, a hypocrite and a liar. Stand up, you bastard evolutionists; stand up with the infidels and atheists, the whoremongers and adulterers!*"

*   *   *

At this point, Doyle turned and said to me over the screaming hysteria of Sunday's audience, "Charles, I think I've heard enough of this drivel. What say we down a couple of pints at the pub?"

"But what of Thackery?" I protested.

"My dear friend, we shall see him soon enough. Right now, I can use a bracer . . . or two."

Two days later I learned of another tragedy while reading the 30 November 1913 edition of the *Uckfield Banner*.

SECOND ATROCIOUS MURDER!

Method matches that used in Ilford

*Barkham Manor handyman found dead
with dagger in his heart*

Police are still puzzled

PILTDOWN, 29 November.—Mr Venus Hargreaves, a hired handyman and resident of Barkham Manor, was found dead to-day by the mistress of the estate, Miss Mabel Kenward.

In a manner completely similar to the recent unsolved murder of Mr Philip Cheswycke of Ilford, Mr Hargreaves was found stabbed in the heart. Also as with the Ilford homicide, Mr Hargreaves' tongue was cut out, placed on his chest, and impaled with a small cross-shaped object.

The local constabulary are at a complete and utter loss as to the identity of the executioner or his motive . . . [etc., etc.]

This meant that Hargreaves was murdered the day after Billy Sunday's sermon. I contacted Doyle immediately.

I had to wait a full week to see him since he was otherwise engaged at a spiritualist convention in London.

"Conan", I said finally, "this is getting very serious. Who will be next? You? Me? Teilhard?—"

"I do not know. But if a tendency can be deduced from only two data points, it seems that those murdered had spoken to one or both of us soon before the act was committed. Perhaps we can make use of this proclivity to smoke out the murderer."

"We must warn the Kenwards," I said urgently. "I have spoken to them countless times and their lives may be in danger as a result."

"Yes, Charles. We must speak to the Kenwards."

We drove over to Barkham Manor late that afternoon. We knocked on the door of the main house and were greeted by its tenant, Robert Kenward.

"Ah, good afternoon, Mr Dawson. What a pleasant surprise to see you again. Come in, please come in."

"Thank you. Nice to see you as well. May I introduce Dr Arthur Conan Doyle?"

"Good afternoon, Dr Doyle. I'm pleased to meet you."

"The pleasure is all mine, Mr Kenward."

"Please, if you will, join me my den where we will be comfortable."

Mr Kenward led us through a rather long hallway, and we entered a corner room to the right. His den was well lit by sunlight which was shining through two large windows. I instantly saw his passion in life, for the room was brimming with golf-clubs, trophies, plaques and other golf miscellanea.

"There is no question, Mr Kenward", I commented, "that you are quite the golf enthusiast. Your collection of antique equipment, to say nothing of your numerous awards, is most impressive, I must say."

"Well, yes, thank you, Mr Dawson", he responded. "Golf *is* a great passion in my life. You know there is a very challenging golf course right here in Piltdown. Perhaps we can play some day."

"Oh, no. I'm afraid not", I said with a chuckle. "I can no better strike a golf-ball than play Doyle's game of three-cushion billiards. I am not a sportsman at all."

Doyle interrupted the small talk. His voice was serious. "I see that you have very recently added yet another trophy to your collection, Mr Kenward—the one prominently displayed on a shelf of its own", he said, pointing to it. "I should think that it has been sitting on the shelf for no more than a day or two, and that you earned it in Scotland, most likely at the Royal and Ancient Golf Club of St Andrews."

"Why, yes, Dr Doyle", Kenward said with a startled smile. "I received it just the other day. How did you know that?"

"Simple. The trophy in question is the only one displayed on which the brass template has not yet acquired a patina. All the others in the room are at least six months old."

"Yes, that is true, but how did you know that I was in Scotland?"

"Simple again. Every year at about this time the Royal and Ancient Golf Club of St Andrews holds an All-Commonwealth amateur tournament. Now, I can see that the blade of your seven-iron"—Doyle removed the club from the golf-bag—"is covered with sand granules as well as grass, Bermuda grass, I believe it is. A seven-iron is used usually from a distance of about one hundred and fifty yards from the green, and then only on a fairway. St Andrews, being a peculiarly Scottish institution, is unique in that it has sandy fairways. All others, particularly those in England, have either grassy fairways or sandy traps, but never a mixture of sand and Bermuda grass. Therefore, you must have competed at St Andrews, the only golf-course where such a combination of materials is used."

I could see that Kenward was stunned.

"Furthermore", Doyle continued, "that remnants of sand, grass and loam still remain on your other clubs indicates to me that you—an avid golfer who would maintain his equipment in top order—have only recently returned with the clubs, and have not had the opportunity to clean them. I would not expect a man such as you, Mr

Kenward, to allow your equipment to remain soiled for more than a day or two. Therefore, you returned from your tournament in Scotland to Piltdown no more than forty-eight hours ago."

"In point of fact, yes, Dr Doyle", said Kenward in agreement. "I left for Scotland on Sunday evening last, and returned only yesterday. I was gone about a week."

With those words and the physical evidence to support them, Kenward evaporated as a suspect.

Still shaking his head in amazement at Doyle's keen perception, Kenward asked, "Incidentally, can I offer you chaps a cup of tea? I would suggest something stronger, but I neither harbour nor partake of spirits."

"A cup of tea will do. And, if you do not mind, we would like to ask you a few questions", I said.

"Of course, Mr Dawson. By the way, terrible thing about Hargreaves. Terrible. I heard about it from my daughter when I returned. He had been employed on the estate since before Mabel and I were living here. Hard worker; devoted to his tasks; fine person. He was a good man, a good man."

"That he was, Kenward."

"Incidentally, we saw you at Billy Sunday's sermon, Mr Kenward", Doyle interjected. "What did you think of it?"

"You were here at the Manor on Sunday last?"

"Yes."

"And you, too, Mr Dawson?"

"Yes, I attended, Kenward."

"How did you know of the meeting?" Kenward asked us quizzically.

"We were informed of it by a friend of ours", Doyle said dryly. "Now, if you will, Kenward, please tell us your reaction to Sunday's oration."

"Oh, praise be to God, absolutely glorious! It was wonderful. That the Lord should bless one of His children as He has done Reverend Sunday is truly a miracle."

Doyle continued his questioning: "It was Barton Thackery, though, who made the arrangements to engage Sunday, was it not?"

"Oh, yes, bless him. Thackery is responsible for the whole of the Sussex congregation. It was very good fortune that he was able to engage Sunday to speak to such a small group of people."

"Is Thackery donating his time to your cause, or is he paid by the congregation?"

"I suppose he is paid, Dr Doyle. We—the membership, that is—make regular monthly donations to the Ilford headquarters."

"Have you ever seen the Ilford office?"

"No, but I imagine that it is very well-appointed, since Thackery and his staff mentioned that they have recently improved the premises."

Improved the premises, indeed! Thackery must have pocketed the blood money. I looked knowingly at Doyle. His mind, too, I am sure, went back to his description of the ramshackle "headquarters" of the Sussex Evangelicals.

"Do you get a regular accounting of funds received and disbursed?"

"No, but . . . well, until recently . . . we had an accountant—a man by the name of Cheswycke—on the staff. Unfortunately, he died recently. Terribly tragic, Doctor." Kenward shifted his line of sight from Doyle's eyes to the floor, and said in a somewhat softer tone of voice: "He was . . . er . . . found in the woods."

"Yes, I've heard about that. Speaking of which, Kenward, what do you make of the severed tongues and the cruciform symbols stuck into them?"

"Tongues? Crosses?"

"Yes. Like Hargreaves, Cheswycke was stabbed in the heart with a dagger, and his tongue was cut out and left on his chest with a small cross stuck into it."

"No, I did not know that. At least I did not know that Cheswycke had died in the same way as Hargreaves. I was told only that he had been murdered whilst walking in the woods."

"And who told you that?"

"Why, Thackery, of course."

"Mm, I see. By the way, we should also like to speak with your daughter, Mabel. It was she, was it not, who first found Hargreaves' corpse?" inquired Doyle.

"Yes, it was, poor girl. The last thing she needed was

to find his body. She has suffered so much stress and strain, and had been so pleased with her success at arranging the hall for Mr Sunday's visit."

"How had she helped to arrange it?"

"Oh, I thought you knew", Kenward said. "Mabel has been a *very* active member of the Sussex Evangelical Association. In fact, she holds a position of very great responsibility. She is an officer—the Secretary/Treasurer—and the only woman on the Board of Directors", he added proudly. "She is charged with handling monetary collection and disbursement."

"Is she now? Well, we should like to speak to her", said Doyle.

"Unfortunately, that would be impossible at the moment, for she is at the Ilford headquarters attending a board meeting."

"*Aha*", I said to myself, "*she must have been present for the meeting at Barkham Manor several weeks before Billy Sunday arrived.*"

"Well, Mr Kenward", Doyle said, "thank you very much for your time. We apologise for the interruption and for any inconvenience we have caused you."

"Not at all, gentlemen. It was a pleasure to see you again, Mr Dawson, and an equal pleasure to have met you, Dr Doyle. Please feel free to attend one of our church services the next time it takes place on the estate. You would be more than welcome. Good-bye and God bless you."

* * *

As we walked back to Doyle's motor, we exchanged the following words:

"Conan, this gets more curious with each day."

"Yes, Charles. More curious but less confounding, for we have reduced the number of suspects. Of course, Hargreaves has been eliminated as a suspect, as has Robert Kenward. And I determined that George Maryon-Wilson, the owner of the Barkham property, has been visiting relatives and otherwise attending to business in Ireland for the past month. That leaves as suspects only Thackery or one of his colleagues—not excluding Mabel Kenward."

"Mabel Kenward!?" I scoffed. "Why, she is the most endearing young thing in the world. My guess is that the most compelling issue in her life is the fact that she is approaching thirty years of age with no husband in sight."

"To the contrary, Charles. I feel certain that Mabel Kenward has no interest whatsoever in marriage at this time. It does appear, however, that she may have more immediate—*and considerably more serious*—concerns."

"But she is a God-loving woman!" I protested.

"Or God-fearing", retorted Doyle without emotion.

"What in God's name are you two doing here?" Thackery screamed as he opened the door to the "headquarters" of the Sussex Evangelical Association.

"Get out . . . Get out! before I call the police!"

"Relax, Mr Thackery", said Doyle in a tranquil tone of voice. "To be sure, it is the police whom you would like to see least of all."

Seated at the table, equally shocked, were another gentleman and none other than Miss Mabel Kenward.

"This is a private establishment", Thackery protested.

"That may indeed be true", responded Doyle, "but murder is a public matter."

Then, looking at the other two in the room, Doyle said to the man, "I remember you, Mr Jonathan Preston." And turning to the lady, "And I am very pleased to meet you, Miss Kenward."

"My friends are none of your business, Doyle", Thackery exploded, "as your friend is none of mine!"

"Ah, but that is not quite true, Mr Thackery. My friend, Charles Dawson by name . . ."

I saw Thackery and Preston flinch at the sound of my name.

". . . is very much part of your business. You have sent him some rather threatening letters, have you not? And you have, in addition, corresponded with another of my friends—Father Teilhard, by name—have you not? I know that I am standing in the same room with a murderer", Doyle added. "I intend to find out who that criminal is. I also intend to prevent further carnage."

"And how do you know", asked Thackery, "that one

of us is a murderer? Did Sherlock Holmes tell you? Or Dr Watson, perhaps? Or maybe that chronic bumbler, Inspector Lestrade, asked you to investigate? Dr Doyle, have you taken it upon yourself to play amateur detective?"

"My good man, I will ignore your child-like remarks", said Doyle. "I have more than a few clues that a murderer is sitting in this very room. First, each of the victims was found with his tongue severed from his mouth. You know your Bible quite well, do you not, Thackery?"

"I am *very* familiar with God's Word."

"Can you quote for me Proverbs, Chapter Ten, Verse Thirty-One?"

I saw anguish appear on Thackery's face.

"Can you quote it for me?" Doyle demanded.

"The mouth of the just bringeth forth wisdom: but the froward tongue shall be cut out."

"Very good, Thackery, very good. And what is that you wear on your lapel?"

"It is a symbol of my devotion to Christ."

"And it is the very same symbol found imbedded in the severed tongues, is it not?"

Silence.

"Is it not, Thackery? Is not that the same type of symbol found imbedded in the tongues?"

At this point, Preston pushed back the chair upon which he was seated out, stood up to what must have been a height of six foot three inches, and faced Doyle.

"And what is it that I can do for you, sir?" inquired Doyle.

Without any response whatsoever, Preston cocked his right arm and threw his fist at Doyle's head. Doyle responded in a flash by blocking the right hand lead with his left arm, and then proceeded to bloody Preston's nose with a quick jab to the face.

Thackery, instantly realising that his man was outclassed, quickly brought the fray to an end.

"*Preston*", he said loudly, "sit down and remain still!"

Preston sat down holding a handkerchief to his crimsoned nose.

"Now, if I may continue", Doyle said impatiently. "Was not each of the victims dispatched quite soon after he had held a conversation with me or with Mr Dawson? And is not the reason for your despicable activities related to the discovery of the Sussex Piltdown Man? You feel threatened, Thackery, do you not? You feel that your fragile house of cards will collapse if word ever gets out among the general public that Man is indeed a product of evolution. You are frustrated because in front of your very eyes you see your power and influence—not to mention your wealth—dissipating. You murdered—and, I am convinced, will continue to murder—to protect your Evangelical charade from further attack. And you rationalise those murders by following literally a document which has been translated from language to language to language over the course of a thousand years, and for which there is not even an original autograph available. How do you know, Thackery, that your King James Version is, in fact, the Word of God? Were the translators as inspired by God as the original authors were? If you have never seen an original document, how can you possibly know that *any* translation is accurate?

"In the final analysis, your belief-system is a swindle, Thackery. A dodge designed to separate your parishioners from their money! There is *no* proof of the Bible's veracity. There is *no* proof of Heaven or Hell; or of salvation, or of the Kingdom of God; or that Christ was crucified, or that Christ was born of a Virgin; or that Christ returned bodily from the dead or, indeed, that Christ even existed. The strongest answer you can give is 'It is true because the Bible says it is so'. But then you are running around in circles, are you not? Because what you are really saying is 'The Bible is the Truth because the Bible says it is the Truth'. You may as well continue to believe in fairies, Thackery, because at one time they seemed the Truth when you found a few pennies under your pillow after the loss of a tooth. But at least *they* graciously retreated along with a recipient's childhood. However, like Peter Pan, you refuse to grow up and step out of your phantasies.

"Face it, Thackery, you and your movement are a fraud. You and the other Evangelical leaders are in it only for the money and the power. You and your Reverend Billy Sunday—he of the Rolls-Royce motor-car—are leeches, sucking dignity, independence and funds from the people you profess to be saving. And you have killed to protect your farcical little empire. I can assure you, Thackery, your crimes will not go unpunished."

I was rapt listening to Doyle. But Thackery had a response at the ready.

"And who are you, Dr Doyle, to pass judgement on right and wrong, good and evil? Who are you to say that Man's law is better than God's? Who are you to tell me what I should believe and how those beliefs should be manifested? God's Truth has served mankind for almost two millennia and he is none the worse for it. Christ has given us a vision of Paradise; He has given us a reason for living . . ."

Doyle interrupted: "Stop, Thackery, *stop!* I am in no mood to hear your Evangelical twaddle."

"No, Doyle, *you* stop. Let us look at what twaddle really is!" Thackery insisted. "Let us look at your evolutionary nonsense. Let us take a close, objective, unbiassed look. I ask you: Does Darwin's theory stand up to the scrutiny of the scientific method? Is evolution *truly* scientific? I submit, sir, that it is not. In fact, it does not even come close. Have you or any other of your apostate fellows ever seen evolution in progress? Have you ever seen one type of animal 'evolve' into another? Of course not. No, Dr Doyle, the secular evolutionists have their own kind of demented scientific method: they build up a mountain of data—much of which is questionable to begin with—and mould . . . and turn . . . and distort those data to suit what they *want to believe* to be the truth. They have no other alternative since no life-form—*no plant and no animal*—can be made or be seen to evolve in the laboratory. Science is supposed to be a system under which experiments are repeatable. Can you repeat what you and your Modernist friends call the evolution of *Eoanthropus* into *Homo*? Of course not; it is impossible! But you *think* that it happened; and you *sense* that it happened; and you force your data to reflect that it happened.

"You cannot *prove* what you believe, Dr Doyle. You take a giant leap of faith from the 'data' and 'evidence' that exist to a conclusion you *want* to believe. What you follow in evolution, I submit, is as much a system of belief as the one that I follow. Evolution is a postulate, and not an observed phenomenon. It has never been witnessed by human observers. It can never be demonstrated in the laboratory!"

"But there is another major difference between our ways of life, belief-systems notwithstanding", protested Doyle vigorously. "My system does not have a thousand-year-long history of treachery, theft, deception and torture. Nor is my system built on the twin pillars of fear and ignorance. There is no occurrence of murder for the cause of the survival of evolutionary theory as there has been and, obviously, continues to be, for the cause of Christianity. I am not required to pray to the God of Evolution as you are to pray to your God in the sky. I am not required to make contributions to the Church of Darwin to save my soul from eternal damnation; nor do I exact indulgences from non-believers in evolution in order to expunge them of 'sin.' I am not afraid of being proven wrong; in fact, Thackery, as a man of science myself, I know of no other way to learn something new. What, over the past two thousand years, have you learned that is new? As far as you are concerned, the Sun still revolves about the Earth; the universe is fewer than six thousand years old; lack of baptism denies one the key to your fictional Heaven; the theatre, music and the other lively arts—the pinnacles of human achievement—should not exist; and babies are born with a yoke of sin as their birthright. And, by your prescription—excuse me: by the *Bible's* prescription—any threat to or transgression from those outdated fossils of belief is punishable by death. In point of fact, Thackery, I am surprised that Cheswycke and Hargreaves were so mercifully slain. Given that Evangelicals eschew the modern, I would have expected them to be burned at the stake, or decapitated, or strangled, or, from your narrow Biblical perspective of justice, taken to a courtyard and *stoned to death!*"

"Don't lecture me about Truth, Doyle!" Thackery exclaimed. "If you want an example of a mangled 'proof' of evolutionary theory, you need look no further than your exalted 'Java Man'. A skull-cap was found by a Dutch physician named Dubois at the bank of the Solo River in the early 'nineties, was it not? As I remember, he estimated the cranial capacity to be about nine hundred cubic centimetres—*from the calvaria alone*! This would be ridiculous enough, Doyle, but for the discovery of a thigh-bone which Dubois *assumed* belonged to the same individual as the skull-cap. These two disparate pieces of anatomy were combined to form a completely new 'missing link', which Dubois called *Pithecanthropus erectus*. Yet this was not sufficient for our wishful Netherlands thinker. No, not enough. For he soon discovered two molar teeth, and seven years later—*seven years later*, Doyle—a premolar, which he claimed to belong to the same specimen. What *proof* is there that all of these little bits and pieces, first of all, were part and parcel of the same individual and, indeed, were not as human as you or I? As all of you evolutionist tricksters do, Dubois used his findings to formulate the conclusion he had firmly fixed in his mind to begin with; that is, to find a 'missing link'. The whole exercise is nonsense!

"And I truly believe, Dr Doyle and Mr Dawson, that the Piltdown Man is of the same fraudulent pedigree. The skull does not belong to the jaw, to which the teeth do not belong. I lend no credence to *Eoanthropus dawsoni*—how clever of you, Mr Dawson!—being a legitimate fossil assemblage. In fact, I doubt even that the component parts of that assemblage are legitimate. It is—and I say this with as much fervour as your attack on Evangelicalism—a fraud! *It is a God-forsaken hoax, Doyle!* And I will either expose it or destroy it. You have met your Dr Moriarty, Doyle. I will not rest until this business is finished."

"You have chosen a formidable opponent, Thackery", Doyle responded. "And that opponent is not only me. You are confronting a scientific community that will never allow the concealment of truth, and that will fight tooth-and-nail any effort to restrict access to knowledge. You and your swindlers will be brought before the law to be tried and convicted of murder, I can assure you."

"I have heard enough, Doyle", spat Thackery. "Preston, show these men out."

Preston stood and pulled a revolver from inside his coat and trained it in our direction.

"This is not the last you will see of me, Thackery", said Doyle calmly. He then turned towards the silent Mabel Kenward.

"And you, Miss Kenward, how do you feel about this issue?"

Mechanically: "I believe that Jesus Christ is God; I believe that He was born of a Virgin; I believe in his substitutionary death; I believe that He rose bodily from the dead; and I believe that He will return in bodily form. And, Dr Doyle, I would *die* to uphold those beliefs."

I asked myself: *"But would she kill?"*

As we departed the "headquarters" under Preston's escort, Doyle said again to Thackery: "You have not seen or heard the last of me and, I can assure you, your sins will not go unpunished."

* * *

"My word, Conan", I said, as we stepped into Doyle's motor, "we could have been killed! These people must be stopped! And", I added, "they know that the Piltdown Man is a fraud."

"*No, they do not!*" Doyle said in rejoinder. "They do not know that; they believe—or want to believe—it is a fraud. They have never seen the material; nor have they attended any of the Society meetings at which it was presented. They know only what they have read in the newspapers, and the Piltdown Man has been sanctioned as legitimate by the press."

"But Thackery seems so knowledgeable about the goings-on in the field of human evolution. How could he know so much?" I asked.

"Because", responded Doyle, "I think he has or, more likely, *had* a somewhat kindred spirit within the Royal Geological Society, a member who would also be a rather more moderate supporter of Evangelicalism, one devoutly believing that God produced the original species but then, having finished His work, retreated from any further intervention, thus allowing life-forms to evolve. Surely, such a person would most logically be our mysterious Mr X."

"And what leads you to that conclusion?" I asked with deep curiosity.

"Elementary, my dear Dawson. Our Mr X is not only knowledgeable about human and ape anatomy, he is also well-versed in the relationship between various fauna and the geological periods during which they lived. The Pliocene/Pleistocene beaver, rhinoceros, deer and elephant bones are cases in point.

"He would have discussed archaeological hoaxes with Thackery during their conversations about Darwinian theory. Thackery may be devious, Charles, but he is not illiterate. Our conversation with him demonstrated the knowledge he has of his enemies. I am sure that at one time he read about what is known as 'The Cardiff Giant'."

"Yes", I said. "Of course! 'The Cardiff Giant'."[87]

"In addition, Charles, our Mr X signed all of his correspondence with the same symbol used by Thackery and company. I think he was trying to accomplish two things. First, for reasons known only to himself, he wanted to participate in our adventure, albeit anonymously. And second, he was trying to warn us of impending danger from the more radical Evangelicals."

"Mr X a Fellow of the Royal Society," I murmured. "Interesting, Conan; how very interesting."

"What is more, Charles, I think that the sequence of events went as follows: Mabel Kenward, an orthodox

---

[87] "The Cardiff Giant" was discovered in October 1869 about three feet underground while a well was being dug in Cardiff, New York, a small upstate farming town. Measuring over ten feet in height and in what was perceived to be a "pertified" condition, the Giant answered the prayers of biblical literalists by substantiating Genesis 6:4 ("There were giants in the earth in those days . . ."). It also lined the pockets of the owner of the land on which it was found—until it was exposed as a giant hoax.

Evangelical, knows that you are working in the gravel-pit at Barkham Manor—she very often sees you digging there in the company of other persons. Mabel is kept up to date on your activities by the local labourer, Hargreaves, whom she has led to believe that her interest in the project is only in passing. Mabel reports your activities to Thackery who, during a general meeting of the Sussex Evangelical Association—which is attended by Mr X— speaks of the evil lurking on the Barkham farm in the guise of three men (Teilhard, Smith Woodward and you) who are digging for fossils. Mr X immediately understands the implications of what Thackery is saying and, by sending you his notes and package, is abetting your deception while warning you of possible danger."

"Fascinating, Conan. *Absolutely fascinating!*" I said.

"Indeed it is, Charles. We must now identify and then speak with Mr X."

We move next to late July, 1914. The site once again is the Barkham Manor gravel-pit, and the incident that I am about to describe began innocently enough as a *bagatelle* designed for my own personal amusement. Smith Woodward and I were digging within the pit when, suddenly, he solicited my attention by pointing out that he had found what he perceived to be a fossil, now broken into two pieces, that appeared to be shaped in the form of a club-like implement. Discovered approximately two feet below the surface (where, of course, I had secreted it), the artifact was surrounded by a clay matrix that immediately enabled Smith Woodward to date it as being contemporaneous with the skull fragments. The two of us began to examine the pieces at the site. Little did I know how much attention and activity would result from my small recreation.

On 2 December 1914 at a meeting of the Geological Society, to which I invited Doyle, the recovered bone implement elicited spirited discussion from a number of members. All agreed the appliance was fashioned by Piltdown Man from a fossilized elephant-bone (indeed, I carved it from an elephant femur—the one included in the package sent to me by Mr X—with the blade of a sharp pocket-knife). One participant proposed that it was a club used as a weapon. Another suggested that it originally had thongs attached to it. A third (Reginald Smith)[88] offered that it "would rank as by far the oldest undoubted sculpture by man in bone". Others, including Mr Lewis Abbott,[89] said that the bone resembled, of all things, a cricket bat, but was certainly used for application other than defending a wicket.

Mr Abbott, a short, stocky man with a ferocious

---

[88] Smith (1874–1940) was an antiquarian with the British Museum.
[89] William Abbott, the jeweler-*cum*-eolithophile, was described by Keith in *The Antiquity of Man* as one "whose opinion in all that pertains to the geology of the Weald deserves serious consideration," p. 296.

moustache, was a strong supporter of the intermediary position of the Piltdown Man in human evolution. His backing of my position was total and unequivocal.

As Abbott was speaking, I saw that Doyle was deep in thought and busy writing something on a sheet of paper. I put on my reading spectacles and peered over to see what was occupying him. What he wrote is shown below in his own handwriting:

Presently, Doyle noticed that I was reading his notes, and he handed me a newspaper clipping from the *Hastings and St Leonards Observer*, dated 1 February 1913. On that date, Abbott had published a short article entitled "Pre-Historic Man: The Newly-Discovered Link in His Evolution". I read it while Abbott had the floor.

The recent discoveries in Sussex have a special bearing on the evolutionary principle. The pit's geological formation is just what had been anticipated, and the fossil fauna just as expected, and the cranium and jawbone most exactly what had been expected in the combination of humanoid, chimpanzoid, and gorilloid features. The jawbone is, as it should be, more like that of a chimpanzee than of a human being, Unfortunately, the part of the jawbone that carries the canine is missing, but if there had been a canine, it would in all probability be essentially chimpanzoid. We have at last discovered the Pleistocene ancestor of at least one branch of modern man.

When I had finished reading, I handed the clipping back to Doyle, who whispered in my ear: "Abbott is Mr X."

I sat through the rest of the meeting in total anxiety, longing for it to end so that, first, Doyle could repeat what he had just said to my incredulous ears and, second, so that I could share my feeling with him that this assemblage, which is considered to be the finest of the world's scientific community, is more gullible and perhaps more feeble-minded than I could ever have imagined.

Herewith, a drawing of the "bone implement", illustratively reimbedded in its elephant-femur source, as published in the March 1915 issue of the *Quarterly Journal of the Geological Society*.

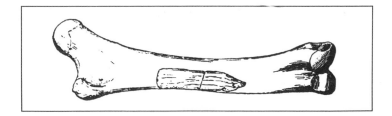

Smith Woodward, in an incredible admixture of arrogance and *naïveté*, was totally convinced of the artifact's authenticity, although I had originally carved it rather nonchalantly to resemble, frankly, I-don't-know-what.

The sham bone implement was the last of the recoveries from the Barkham Manor gravel-pit. I never returned there again.[90]

"Conan", I said excitedly as we left the chamber, "did you say to me during the meeting that Abbott is Mr X?"

"Yes, I did, Charles."

"How do you know?"

"The newspaper article betrayed him."

"In what way? How, Conan?" I pleaded.

"Simple mathematics, Charles. The article was published on 1 February 1913, meaning that Abbott had to prepare it for the editorial staff sometime in January, or possibly even earlier than that. I checked the Geological Society register and learned that he did not sign it on 18 December 1912, the date when Smith Woodward and you presented the bone fragments and their reconstruction to the Society. Now, the paper you and Smith Woodward presented was not published in the Society *Journal* until

---

[90] Smith Woodward, however, would continue to search within and around it for years to come.

March of 1913, so Abbott could not have known the contents of your presentation until then. In addition, he could not have seen casts of the reconstruction since they were not available until April. He also could not have seen the 'chimpanzoid' canine because Teilhard would not 'find' that until August 1913. Abbott therefore had information that should not have otherwise have been available to him when he was writing his article. In the article, Abbott mentions 'a chimpanzoid jaw now before me'. He also mentions 'a row of human jaws now before me', and that there are 'thousands' of jaws in his collection. The orang-utan jawbone which you received in the package sent to you must have come from Abbott's own private collection."

"By Jove, I believe you are correct, Conan!" I said. "Your powers of deduction are at least as good as those of Sherlock Holmes", I added with a smile. "When I showed Teilhard the contents of the package and the letter sent to me, neither of us had even the vaguest idea who might have sent them. It makes perfect sense that Abbott is our man!"

"Yes, I think so, Charles. But we must speak to Abbott himself in order to substantiate the hypothesis. Can you arrange for us to visit him?"

"Of course. I've known Abbott for many years and he is a good friend."

*   *   *

On 10 August 1914, tragic events suddenly moved domestic, if not international, interest away from the pinpoint on the map called Piltdown.

On that day, England and France entered into a declared state of war with Austria-Hungary and, by extension, with that country's ally, Germany. The whole social, economic and, certainly, military, structure of Great Britain had changed virtually overnight.[91] Teilhard had gone home to his native France to join the army.

On 2 February 1915, I received a letter from him:

> My dear friend Charles:
>   I am writing you from a small town called Zuydcoote, not too far from the town of Dunkerque near the France-Belgium border. I am sorry I could not write to you sooner, but I have been moving from place to place since 20th January, when I arrived at the Front.
>   War is indeed hell on earth. Although I could easily have avoided active service and could certainly have side-stepped

---

[91] Arthur Keith, in the third impression of the first edition (July 1915) of his classic *Antiquity of Man*, wrote an "Additional Note to Preface": "A year has passed since the proof of this book was corrected and its preface written. The events of the year have revolutionised the outlook of all of us; we have burst suddenly into a critical phase in the evolutionary progress of mankind; we have had to lay aside the problems of our distant past and concentrate our thoughts and energies on the immediate present. Liège and Namur, which figure in this book as sites of peaceful antiquarian discovery, have become the scenes of bloody war. And yet, amidst all the distractions of the present time, the author hopes there may be some who will wish to survey the issues of the present fateful period from the the distant standpoint of a student of man's early evolution. It is in such a hope that this book is now put forth."

duty in the arenas of conflict, I was not able to abandon my love for France. I am employed as a *bancardier*—a stretcher-bearer! I wear the *képi* and blue uniform of the French infantry in contrast to the khaki worn by the Tunisians with whom we are allied.

Of course, I have war stories to tell like any other man in my circumstance. To wit: I recently celebrated Mass in a rat-infested shelter so low that I was obliged to officiate kneeling. As I was putting away the sacred vessels and vestments, a shell exploded nearby. No one was hurt.

It is now the end of a long day and, against my better judgement (no, Charles, *as a function of* my better judgement), I accepted a pint of whisky from an officer-friend of mine. I am sipping directly from the small bottle as I write this letter. I am tired, Charles, so tired; and I wish you were with me—no!—I wish that I were with you. But I shall not—cannot!—rest until my work at the Front is done.

At twilight today I had walked up to the top of the hill from which there was a general view of the sector we had just left and to which we would shortly, no doubt, be returning. Stretched out before me lay rough meadow-lands wreathed in the mist that was now forming and in the elbow-bends of the river curved into mild white splashes; beyond, the bare ridge stood out, sharp as a knife-edge, against the golden sunset, dotted with *drachen* [kite-balloons]. At intervals a mine sent up a plume of smoke into the silence.

When I am in the front-line, I am frightened of the shelling, just as everyone else is. Like everyone else, I count the days until our relief, and I watch carefully for the signs that announce its arrival. When we "go down the line", no one is more delighted than I am. Every time this happens I feel that this time I have at last had enough, and more than enough, of the trenches and war. As recently as this afternoon, I was still drinking in the joy of living again, with no nagging at the back of my mind, in the warm embrace of innocent nature. I was savouring the bliss of stretching out beneath the trees and of allowing their foliage to be reflected in a completely relaxed and carefree mind.

And now, as always, I find myself turning back instinctively towards the Front and the fighting!

Is it not ridiculous to be so drawn into the magnetic field of the war as to be unable to spend a week in the rear without scanning the horizon, as one scans a well-loved sea-strand, for the motionless line of "sausage-balloons"? To be so hypnotized as to be unable suddenly to glimpse at night the silvery spark of a swooping flare, or even its reflection in the clouds, without feeling my heart beat faster, without a sense of regret, without hearing a summons?

More than ever, on this particular evening, in this wonderfully calm and stimulating setting—in which I am sheltered from the violent emotions and intolerable strain of the trenches and can feel the impressions that the war has sunk deep into my being emerge with new vigour—now more than ever the Front casts its spell over me.

What, then, when you consider it closely, are the properties peculiar to this fascinating and deadly line? By what hidden power does it attach itself to all that is most alive in my being—and so irresistibly draw it to itself?

Since, at this particular moment, I can look around me with greater calm and a more penetrating eye, I must try to analyse myself more clearly than I have ever done before. I must know.

For my own part I can say that without war there would be a world of feelings that I would never otherwise have known or suspected. Nobody except those who were there will ever have the wonder-laden memory that a man can retain of the plains, when the air stank of chlorine and the shells were tearing down the poplars along by the canal—or, again, of the charred hillsides when they held the odour of death. Those more than human hours impregnate life with a clinging, ineradicable flavour of exaltation and initiation, as though they had been transferred into the absolute. When I look back, all the magic of the East, all the spiritual warmth of Paris are not worth the mud of Douaumont.

Please excuse my presumptive meandering, dear Charles. However, the closeness I feel for you permits me, I pray, to reveal my feelings. But so much for my imposition.

Here is an interesting story: One day while I was washing my linen in the pond of a farm near the Belgian frontier, I was found by a corporal of the colonial infantry. I recognised him; "Max Bégouën?" I enquired. "That's my name," he responded. "I'm Teilhard." "Ah!" said Bégouën, "you're the Piltdown man."

What of Sussex Man, Charles?

Please send my regards to Doyle and my fondest wishes and love to Hélène.

I remain your faithful friend and companion,

Pierre

The War, of course, became the immediate—and almost exclusive—subject of conversation among my friends and associates every time we met. Doyle, who assiduously followed the activities at the various fronts, was a constant companion during these tumultuous times.

A portrait of the "Piltdown men," painted by the artist John Cooke, was unveiled to the public at the Royal Academy's annual exhibition in May 1915. A photograph

of Cooke's artistry is shown above. Represented in the portrait are: in the front row from left to right, Arthur Underwood, Arthur Keith, William Pycraft and Edwin Ray Lankester; in the back row from left to right, Frank Barlow, Grafton Elliot Smith, myself, and Smith Woodward. Note the image of Charles Darwin on the wall behind, peering down upon the group.

This group, and others in several countries—but particularly in England and the United States—had achieved a surprising degree of notoriety among the non-scientific community. The portrait of the Piltdown men, having been reproduced in the pages of *The Illustrated London News*, assigned faces to the names that were becoming more and more recognised outside Academia. In fact, the ancient Man of Sussex had become popularised to such an extent that The Lamb was renamed "The Piltdown Man."

The controversy was being discussed in every corner of the world, reaching all the Continental and North American countries, as well as Australia.

I was tickled by the knowledge that "Charles Dawson" had become a name known the world over and that my likeness in Cooke's painting was being splashed internationally. These were, indeed, heady times for me.

The following brief summary illustrates the hodge-podge of positions that had been assumed with respect to the bones and eoliths by mid-1915.

Osborn[92]: Canine is an upper, not lower, tooth. Both Smith Woodward's and Keith's reconstructions are in error.

Smith[93]: Smith Woodward's reconstruction is correct.

Lankester[94]: Not convinced that the eoliths or the bone implement were fashioned by Piltdown Man.

Keith: Brain-case and jaw *may* belong to the same creature. Eoliths and bone implement both man-made.

---

[92] Henry Fairfield Osborn (1857–1935) was Director of the American Museum of Natural History. He eventually became a monist.

[93] Dawson is referring to Grafton Elliot Smith.

[94] Edwin Ray Lankester—see note 66.

Lyne[95]: Canine does not belong to the mandible, but the mandible belongs to the skull.

Miller[96]: Jaw is not human, but an ape's. Canine is upper, not lower, tooth. Brain-case is *Homo*. Jaw is type specimen for a new chimpanzee species, *Pan vetus*.

Underwood[97]: Agrees with Keith; disagrees with Lyne.

The antagonism brought about by the diversity of views among the scientists was becoming something of a concern to me since, at certain points, opinions that were diametrically opposed to those I wanted advertised had become rather strongly advocated. In addition, some "unfriendly" positions were beginning to be shared by too large a number of scientists to satisfy my well-being. I had to bring the debate back onto the track, as it were. Dramatic new "evidence" was required to meet that end.

On 4 January 1915, in the grounds of Sheffield Park—about two miles north of Piltdown Common—I "found" more evidence of Sussex Man. The "discoveries" I made were designed to be interpreted as the remains of a second *Eoanthropus* individual. On 9 January 1915, I wrote to Smith Woodward:

---

[95] W. Courtney Lyne (?–1949) was a dentist.

[96] Gerrit S. Miller (1869–1956) was a mammologist at the Smithsonian Institution.

[97] Arthur Swayne Underwood (1854–1916) was a professor of dental surgery.

I believe we are in luck again! I have got a fragment of the left side of a frontal bone with a portion of the orbit and root of [the] nose. Its outline is nearly the same as your original restoration and being another individual the difference is very slight. . . . [T]he general colour and condition much the same as *Eoanthropus*. The forehead is quite angelic!

On another occasion, I "recovered" an occipital fragment and a molar tooth from the same Sheffield Park site (the occipital piece was from the original skull; the molar tooth was the rear-most one which I had removed from the orang-utan jaw two and a half years earlier). A strategically-placed rhinoceros molar fragment allowed Smith Woodward to date the remains. Since the new finds have not yet been formally presented to the scientific community, I have no idea whether or not they will be favourably received.[98] I can only hope that these new remains will reinforce the position of Smith Woodward in regard to Sussex Man, as well as that of those who currently agree with him.

In late April, I arranged an appointment for Doyle to visit Lewis Abbott with me at his jeweller's shop at 8,

---

[98] The Sheffield Park remains were not presented to the Geological Society until February 28, 1917, six months after Dawson died. At that meeting Smith Woodward said: "From the facts now described, it seems reasonable to conclude that *Eoanthropus dawsoni* will eventually prove to be as definite and distinct a form of early Man as was at first supposed; for the occurrence of the same type of frontal bone with the same type of lower molar in two

Grand Parade, in Hastings. I did not let on to Abbott the true reason for our visit; I told him only that we should like to discuss the Piltdown Man with him. We were greeted warmly as we entered his establishment.

"Well done, pip-pip, here-here! and all that, Charles. You and Smith Woodward have done a splendid job with Sussex Man. I am delighted to consider myself one of your most ardent supporters", Abbott said, after our handshakes and his introduction to Doyle. "And I am delighted to make your acquaintance, Dr Doyle. I am an incurable devotee of your Sherlock Holmes adventures."

"Well, thank you very much, Abbott", Doyle responded. "You know of course that I have written on other subjects as well. The problem is, nobody seems to want anything other than Sherlock Holmes. I'm afraid that some day I may have to kill him off."

"Ah, my dear Dr Doyle, you tried that once and it did not last very long, did it now?"[99]

"No, it did not. And I am certain that I have you either to thank or, perhaps, to blame to some extent for his reappearance", said Doyle in good humour.

"I will graciously accept your thanks", said Abbott with

---

separate localities adds to the probability that they belonged to one and the same species."

[99] In "The Adventure of the Final Problem" (published in *The Strand* in December 1893), readers are led to believe that both Holmes and Moriarty plunged to their deaths from a narrow path overlooking a chasm. Popular demand resurrected the famous detective.

a short bow and a smile. "Now, I will prepare us some tea whilst you explain the reason for this pleasant surprise."

"You are aware, Lewis, are you not, of the deaths of Mr Philip Cheswycke, of Ilford, and Mr Venus Hargreaves, who worked at the Barkham farm?" I asked.

"Yes, I am. Poor chaps."

"How well did you know Cheswycke?" I asked.

"What!"

"How well did you know Philip Cheswycke, Lewis?"

"Well . . . er . . . I . . ."

"Come now, Abbott", Doyle said reassuringly, "there is nothing to fear."

Abbott cleared his throat. "I knew him quite well."

"You were acquainted with him through your dealings with the Sussex Evangelicals, is that not correct?" said Doyle.

"Why, yes. How in Heaven's name did you know that?"

"We followed a long and circuitous route to learn it, Abbott", Doyle responded. "We also know that you are Mr Dawson's artifactual benefactor. We know that it was you who sent him the package of fossils and other relics, along with the 'Dancing Men' notes and other communications signed with a cross."

"How could you possibly . . . ?"

"No matter, Abbott. You are not in any trouble. We are merely here to prevent any more murders. Incidentally, how is it you knew that Dawson's Piltdown activities were fraudulent?"

"Oh, simple enough," Abbott responded. "As you know, the Sussex Evangelical Association has held more than several meetings at the Barkham farm. One day, while I was in attendance at one of the gatherings I saw Charles working in the gravel-pit by the side of the road. As I was casually watching him, it struck me as rather queer that he would remove an object from his utility bag and bury it amongst the gravels. I realised at that point that something was amiss."

"Mm, I see", Doyle said. "You are very observant."

"Indeed you are," I mentioned in agreement. "However, be that as it may, Lewis, you can help us immeasureably by explaining to us the difference between your Evangelical faction and that of Thackery."

"You know Thackery?"

"Yes, Abbott", said Doyle. "We know him very well."

"Gentlemen, I am truly amazed at what you know. Truly amazed. I will tell you all. Please make yourselves comfortable.

"I was raised in a remote part of Essex known as the Dengie Hundred. While living there as a young man I was a frequent speaker at outdoor meetings defending orthodox religious views, but at one meeting a person in the audience asked some awkward questions based on geology, of which I knew nothing; so I made up my mind to learn. My interest in geology paid off when, in the early 'nineties, I discovered a rather large number of fossil

Pleistocene species in the Igtham shode[100] fissures, for which I was graciously given a share of the Lyell Award by the Royal Geological Society.

"I moved to Sevenoaks to be nearer my digging activities, and opened my jewellery business here in Hastings. It was during this period that I was fortunate enough to have discovered the Hastings midden-heaps.[101]

"It was also around this time that I met Barton Thackery. He was involved with organising and building up his fledgling Sussex Evangelical Association. The circumstances under which we met were quite unusual. He was scheduled to give a talk in Hastings on Biblical inerrancy. My interest in the topic, coupled with the proximity of the lecture to my home in Hastings, eased my decision to attend. I was also curious about the subject matter of his presentation: he was to speak about navels, of all things!"

"Navels?" I echoed with a puzzled frown.

"Yes, Charles, navels. It seems that, in addition to discovering how many angels could dance on the head of a pin, one of the issues that was pushing theology to its exegetical limits was the question of whether or not Adam had a navel."

---

[100] A "shode" or "shoad" is a dialectical English term that means a fragment of vein material removed by natural agencies from an outcrop, and lying in the surface soil or debris.
[101] A midden is an accumulation of dwelling refuse.

I glanced at Doyle, who seemed to be as perplexed as I was. Obviously, Abbott also saw Doyle's expression and smiled at him.

"Yes, Dr Doyle, the subject of Thackery's speech was Adam's navel. The issue was this: an Adamic navel would have been an unnecessary bodily adjunct since God created him as a flawless human being. Why would a divinely-created, perfect—and parentless—creature need a navel? Indeed, why would *any* placental mammal need one if it was created *ex nihilo* by God?

"Now, some people argue that, even if Adam *did* have a navel, he must have been a perfect creation, albeit with the *appearance* of having had human parentage. But then the question becomes: Why would God want to create Adam to *seem* to have had a mother and father? Perhaps, some suggested, to make Adam and the world he lived in appear ancient when in fact it is actually no older than several thousand years. In other words, God must have created a world having the *appearance* of great age.

"This issue of Adam's navel is not new at all. You are both familiar with the many classical paintings of Adam and Eve in the Garden of Eden. You are also familiar with the strategically-placed fig-leaves, which all artists used to cover up the first couple's private parts. Sexual inhibition notwithstanding, there is no artistic agreement about what Adam and Eve really looked like. Thus, there are some paintings that show the pair as having navels, there are some paintings that show the pair as having no navels, and there are some paintings that avoid addressing the issue altogether by showing a small twig or twining vine that covers up the part of the body where a navel would exist."

"I have never given so much as the slightest thought to that", I said.

"Many persons do not", Abbott responded. "In fact, most do not. The exceptions, however, are the Thackerys of the world. And Thackery has a long intellectual lineage. Back in 1857 a chap named Philip Henry Gosse[102]—a Plymouth Brother and devout Biblical literalist—confronted the navel problem and wrote his conclusions in a tract entitled *Omphalos*. *Omphalos* is, of course, the Greek word for 'navel'. Since Gosse was a supporter of Biblical inerrancy and a believer in an all-powerful and perfect God, he could not accept the idea that the Lord's creations could have imperfections, such as a missing navel. Gosse believed that Adam must have had a navel. But, then, he asked, *Why would Adam need one?* This was the enigma that he dealt with."

"And how did he resolve that conundrum?" Doyle asked.

"By suggesting that life was a circular process rather than a linear one. Life, said Gosse, was an unbroken chicken-to-egg-to-chicken-to-egg series; or, if you want,

---

[102] 1810–1888.

an oak-to-acorn-to-oak-to-acorn series. Now, if a perfect God created all placental creatures as perfect adults, the first of them must have had navels. However, the navels, said Gosse, are *representatives* of species continuity through what he termed a 'prochronic' existence—that is, existence outside of time, before the physical act of creation. Every other part of the body—Adam's body less his navel, in this case—Gosse labelled as 'diachronic,' existing in actual time. God knew that human beings after Adam and Eve would need to have navels. So He built into the first couple the ability to meet that requirement. The navel next appeared in Cain and Abel and, subsequently, in every other human being since then.

"*Now*", Gosse argued, "it made no difference whether God created the chicken first or the egg first. For, if He created the chicken first, the ovum would be prochronic: it would have existed as part of the chicken at the moment of creation. If God created the egg first, the *chicken* would have been prochronic, and would have contained all of the chemistry and mechanism for producing another egg."

"Aha", I said, "thus God initiated *two* types of existence—one that gives the appearance of temporal linearity, prochonic existence; and the other as a sequential process in actual time, diachronic existence. One of His creations was Adam's prochronic navel. That removed the seeming contradiction from God's activities."

"Precisely, Charles", said Abbott. "Getting back to Thackery, he presented the Gosse position to his audience. But in doing so, he unwittingly attacked the venerable Victoria Institute of London, of which he was a member. The Institute had historically been an association comprising British Biblical literalists. Its purpose was to discuss and propagandise the most conservative of Christian dogma. However, by and by they had slowly but inexorably begun to move further and further from orthodoxy to a more liberal Evangelical position. It is in support of that more moderate position that I belong to the Institute. But Thackery abandoned his membership out of frustration—and out of anger, I must add—and joined up with a new organisation called the Evolution Protest Movement. It was at this point that the Sussex Evangelicals, too, suffered a philosophical schism. And we are obviously still in the throes of reconciling those differences."

"I see now", said Doyle slowly. "So *that* is the origin of the orthodox/moderate split in the Association."

"Yes, Dr Doyle, you are correct. Thackery on the one side, and myself on the other. Yet, for all my interest in geology and archaeological artifacts, I never lost my faith in Jesus Christ as Lord, despite my strong belief that evolution had occurred and still occurs, and despite my belief in Uniformitarianism.[103] I believe that evolution and Christianity are not mutually exclusive."

---

[103] *Uniformitarianism* is a geological doctrine which states that existing processes are acting in the same manner with essentially the same intensity as

"Teilhard—you know of Teilhard, I am sure—holds a similar opinion", I said.

"Yes, I know. I have read many of his writings and I admire the man immensely."

"Please continue, Abbott", Doyle said.

"I still feel strongly that the universe in general and life on Earth in particular are of divine origin. I have always believed that. I believe that after God created the various kinds—of which there were many fewer at the moment of creation than there are today—He infused in those kinds a mechanism which allowed them to become as much one with nature as possible. In order to do that, the various flora and fauna had to be given the ability to change in response to a changing environment. The mechanism for change—a God-given mechanism, mind you—is descent through modification, evolution. God created and infused the mechanics; and Darwin learned what they are and explained them in his *Origin* for the world to understand."

Abbott stood to refill our tea-cups.

"Now, what all of this means to me is that the Biblical narrative cannot be taken as a *literal* explanation for the

---

they did in the past, and that this is sufficient to account for all geological changes. This model is in direct contradiction to the doctrine of *catastrophism*, which states that changes in the Earth's crust have in the past been brought about suddenly by physical forces [read "God"] operating in ways that cannot be observed today. The Noachian Flood is considered to be an example of catastrophism.

existence of *all* natural phenomena", he went on. "Thus, the Sussex Evangelicals split, with Thackery and his followers having moved to one side of the argument, the orthodox position, and I and supporters of my point of view having moved to the other, which allows for evolution."

"I assume", said Doyle, "that Cheswycke was a member of your moderate camp."

"Oh, no, Dr Doyle. Not at all", said Abbott emphatically. "Cheswycke was among the most ardent orthodox Evangelicals in that group. He was also a member of the Evolution Protest Movement as well as an *Omphalos* supporter. His problem lay in other areas. One of them was . . . well . . . not knowing when to remain silent. Although I am not aware of the specific circumstances, I am sure that he is dead today because of something he said to outsiders of the movement that was perceived by the extremists as being threatening to their cause. No, gentlemen, Cheswycke was an honorable man; he would never stray from the strait and narrow."

"Very interesting, Abbott. Very interesting indeed", said Doyle. "Tell us now, if you will, of Mabel Kenward."

"Ah, Mabel Kenward. Sweet, sweet Mabel Kenward. A wolf in sheep's clothing, if you ask me. Fanatic to the extreme. Biblical literalist, anti-Modernist, anti-evolutionist, anti-Catholic. Anti-Semitic, anti-Negro, anti-Irish. Anti-anything-she-is-not. Anti-everything-but-herself."

"Anti-Labour?" asked Doyle facetiously as he stood up from his chair.

Following Doyle's lead, I said, "Lewis, we have taken much of your time with our numerous questions, and I want to thank you for assisting me in this Piltdown affair. However, I am sure you understand the jeopardy you may have put yourself in. Thackery and his gang of thugs will obviously stop at nothing. How are you going to protect yourself from his wrath?"

"Not to worry, Charles", Abbott said with a grin. "After Cheswycke's death—which, upon reading about the dagger and the cross-impaled tongue, I instantaneously knew was at the hand of the extremists—I surreptitiously recovered all of his financial records from his desk-drawer at the Ilford headquarters. Thackery is aware that those records—with his signatures on them—are secured under lock and key in a safe-deposit vault, with instructions to give the contents to the police in the event of my untimely death. If I live to a ripe old age and the vault is opened and the contents read, the reader will know only that the Sussex Evangelical Association—and Thackery, in particular—were cowardly thieves. And there will be no mention of your escapade. Piltdown Man and I are safe, Charles. And Thackery—may God forgive him!—knows it."

"Well, Abbott, thank you for your time, the information, and the tea", said Doyle. "We apologise for the imposition."

"My pleasure", said Abbott with a smile. "My pleasure indeed."

On our way back to Doyle's motor I asked: "What now, Sherlock?"

"We shall make an unannounced social call on our sweet Miss Mabel Kenward."

We motored from Hastings to the Barkham farm. During the ride, I said to Doyle: "I think we have found our murderer, Conan. It is clear from our conversation with Abbott that Thackery is our man. He had the motive, and the *modus operandi* for each murder points directly at him."

"That does appear to be so, Charles. However, although Thackery may have been the brains behind the criminal acts, he may not have been the brawn. We are not quite finished with this case."

We arrived at the farm and walked directly towards the Manor House, where Mabel Kenward resided. We were directed to her chamber by a domestic day-worker. Doyle rapped on her closed door.

When she opened the door and recognised us, there was a repetition of the cold welcome we had been afforded at Ilford.

"I am in no mood for visitors, gentlemen. Please go away and leave me be", were her first words.

"Indeed, Miss Kenward, we shall reinforce your desire

not to see us", Doyle responded as he dispassionately pushed his way into the room. I followed him in, rather embarrassed by our intrusion.

Her room, which doubled as a bedroom and study, was neatly arrayed. Several framed Biblical quotations hung on the wall. There was also a signed photograph of Billy Sunday, under which one of his quotations was suspended: "WHEN THE WORD OF GOD SAYS ONE THING AND SCHOLARSHIP SAYS ANOTHER, SCHOLARSHIP CAN GO TO HELL". Like a bloodhound, Doyle strode past the bed to the desk, which was piled high with several books and a stack of pamphlets entitled *The Fundamentals*.

"How *dare* you intrude on my private quarters!" she expostulated. Then, turning towards Doyle: *"Get away from my desk!"*

"This will not take very long, Miss Kenward", said Doyle firmly. "In fact, we should be leaving in just a few minutes."

Miss Kenward stood defiantly, arms crossed in front of her chest.

"What, may I ask, are these?" Doyle enquired, as he held two newspaper clippings aloft.

"That, sir, is none of your business."

"It *is* my business, Miss Kenward. It is very much my business. I have seen these before. They are newpaper articles reporting the murders of Philip Cheswycke and Venus Hargreaves. Why do you keep them?"

Silence.

"It was you who found Hargreaves' corpse in his quarters, was it not, Miss Kenward? The newspaper article says as much."

Silence.

"Yet, as far as I know, the police have not even questioned you in any great detail about his murder; is that not so, Miss Kenward?"

Silence.

"You took advantage of your physical charm and Hargreaves' gentility and gullibility to gain access to his quarters after having learned from him that he invited Mr Dawson and me to hear Billy Sunday's sermon, did you not, Miss Kenward? And you seduced him to the point where you kissed him, and implanted in him the expectation of love-making; did you not, Miss Kenward?"

Still silence.

"And when he was made to feel comfortable with your advances, you withdrew a dagger from under your clothing and stabbed him in the heart. You then severed his tongue and impaled it with one of *these!*" Doyle said as he grabbed a handful of lapel-pin crosses from atop Miss Kenward's desk.

"I resent your accusation, Dr Doyle", Miss Kenward finally said. "What proof at all do you have that I was with Hargreaves on the day he died?"

"You know that I have acquaintances at Scotland Yard", said Doyle, as he slowly began to pace around the room, hands clasped behind his back. "They directed me to the local constabulary, who directed me to the local morgue, where I viewed Hargreaves' body."

I saw Miss Kenward's face flush red as Doyle surveyed the items on top of the dressing-table.

"While examining the corpse, I noted that his shirt bore traces of cosmetics . . ."

"I do not use cosmetics", Miss Kenward interrupted.

Almost ignoring her words, Doyle continued: "I cut off a piece of his shirt on which remained some lipstick and the odour of bottled scent."

"I do not use lipstick or scent", Miss Kenward protested once again.

"Then what is *this?*" Doyle asked swiftly, as he lifted a small cylinder from the table. "No need to answer, Miss Kenward. It is a lipstick"—Doyle examined it closely—"and I can see that it appears to have been used perhaps two or three times since the smooth surface is barely disturbed. It was used once or twice so that a lady unaccustomed to painting her lips (such as you) could practise applying it, and a third time when you employed it in earnest before visiting Hargreaves in his quarters."

"I did no such thing."

"Come now, you must admit, Miss Kenward, that it is highly unusual—indeed, contrary to what you believe—for a practising Evangelical to own a lipstick. You would agree with that, would you not, Miss Kenward?"

"I admit to nothing."

"Of course, of course. Nor would you admit that a

person of your religious persuasion would use bottled scent," Doyle said as he held up an ampule between his fingers. He removed the cap and sniffed the contents. "I must confess, Miss Kenward, that this fragrance appears identical to that on Hargreaves' shirt. And I assure you that Scotland Yard's Criminal Investigation Department can match the residue of these cosmetics to those in your possession now."

"Nonsense!" protested Miss Kenward. "Any woman could have left your supposed evidence."

"I have proof that it was yours."

"You have *no* proof!"

"My dear", Doyle stated in an almost off-handed way, "I even have proof that you *kissed* Venus Hargreaves."

"What is that?"

"Yes, I can demonstrate beyond doubt that you kissed Mr Hargreaves on the day you murdered him."

"I did not kiss and I did not murder Mr Hargreaves!"

"Unfortunately, you are quite wrong there, Miss Kenward. Quite wrong", said Doyle in a serious voice. "I have *indisputable* proof that you did. And you left the evidence, along with the lipstick and perfume, on Hargreaves' shirt.

"You may know", he continued, "that the C.I.D. has discovered three methods for unequivocal identification of persons. The first is the fingerprint: no two people have exactly the same pattern. The second is the ear: no two people have exactly the same structure and shape. And the third . . . well, the third, young lady, is the topology of the human lips. When pursed, as during a kiss, the shape of the lips, coupled with the pattern of the furrowing, is unique to an individual. Mine are unique, Dawson's are unique. Your lips, Miss Kenward, are unique. And I have in my possession a perfect impression of your lips on the scrap of Hargreaves' shirt. I have the *corpus delicti*."

Mabel Kenward—and I—stared at Doyle in frozen awe.

"And now, my dear sweet lass, would you care to apply the lipstick one last time?" Doyle withdrew a small edition of the New Testament from his inside coat pocket. "Would you care to kiss the only thing you *truly* love?"

"No, no", protested Miss Kenward, now breathing erratically and breaking down into tears.

I gave her my handkerchief.

"What is to become of me?"

"That is up to you", Doyle responded. "First, however, you must answer two questions. Number one: Are there plans to assassinate either Mr Dawson or Father Teilhard?"

Miss Kenward look up with tears in her eyes and said, almost in a whisper, "Yes."

I felt my mouth go dry and my forehead break out in perspiration.

"Tell me about that", Doyle demanded.

"Teilhard will be killed on the Front in France by one

of our men. I should think that the assassination will take place any day now."

"And who is this man?" Doyle asked.

"I do not know", Miss Kenward responded.

"You do know, Miss Kenward!" Doyle shouted. "And you will supply me with the information now, or I shall have no other choice than to speak to Scotland Yard?!"

Silence.

"Who is the assassin, Miss Kenward?"

Doyle stood up to his full six feet two inches. Towering over the diminutive Miss Kenward, he grabbed her by the shoulders and shook her stiffly. *"Who is the man we want?"*

Finally giving in to the unrelenting pressure, Miss Kenward screeched: *"Preston. It is Jonathan Preston you want!"*

Doyle released Miss Kenward and paced the floor deep in thought. "And what of Mr Dawson?" he asked the tormented young lady.

Miss Kenward looked up at me with anguish in her face and whimpered, "You will die, too. And I cannot tell you any more because I do not know any more."

I wanted a whisky then more than I had ever done in my life. Unfortunately, Miss Kenward, being an orthodox Evangelical, was unlikely to have any at the ready.

"What is to become of me, now that I have given you the information you wanted, Dr Doyle?" Miss Kenward asked.

"I am a man of my word", Doyle responded. "I shall keep the piece of Hargreaves' shirt under lock and key, assuming that you will never—*ever*!—speak of the Piltdown affair again. If word gets out that you did speak of it, I shall turn the evidence of your guilt over to Scotland Yard. The site of the evidence will be told to a person unknown to you, and he will be instructed to place the shirt scrap into the custody of the police in the event of my untimely death. Is this agreement clear to you, Miss Kenward?"

"Yes, it is."

"Then we shall leave you alone, but not, I am sure, in peace."

As we were leaving Barkham Manor, Doyle turned to me and said, "I have been asked by the Foreign Office to go on a tour of inspection on the Continent. I shall be travelling under the auspices of the *Daily Chronicle* to write a series of eye-witness articles about the war fronts.[104] Since I will be visiting the French lines, I shall leave immediately to see if I can get any information about Teilhard. I will stay in touch with you and will fill you in on the particulars when I return."

Doyle left for the Continent the following day. Two days after that, I received another letter from Teilhard:

---

[104] Doyle was accompanied by Robert Donald, the editor of the newspaper.

My dear friend Charles,

I must tell you of a frightening experience I had this week. I was at the Front near Verdun, where I was carrying out my duties as *bancardier*. During the nightmare of a raging battle, I and another stretcher-bearer were rushing an injured comrade to the hospital tent. I had the forward position and my partner took up the rear on this mission of mercy. Running towards us from the distance came another soldier, brandishing a cocked side-arm. The madness in his glazed eyes became evident as he approached. Nearing the stretcher, the assassin screamed: *"Die, Heretic Teilhard! Die in the name of Jesus!"* He fired one shot as he rushed past us, but, due to his inability to aim with precision, he killed the wrong bearer.

With an almost eerie lack of emotion, I held firm and did not drop my end of the stretcher as I watched the injured man slide slowly onto the blood-soaked corpse. The wounded soldier's body crumpled and lay in a twisted heap; then he, too, expired.

I believe that on this day I said the most fervent Mass of my life. As I preached to my congregation of soldiers, "I would rather have handled a machine gun than a stretcher, since it seems to me that this is quite appropriate for a priest. Isn't a priest supposed to bear the sorrows of the world in whatever form they present themselves?"

Take care of yourself, Charles.

Warmest regards to Doyle, and all my love to Hélène.

Pierre

I never saw Teilhard again, but a week later, I received a telegraph wire from Doyle. His correspondence contained three extremely comforting words: *"Teilhard is alive!"* I could not wait to hear his story.

*   *   *

I am quite ill as I prepare this reminiscence. In fact, it is this reason, in particular, which brings me to write this memoir at the present time. I have been diagnosed by my Dr Fawssett as having what he characterises as "an anaemic condition." In addition, my physician tells me that I am suffering from pyorrhoea alveolaris.[105] I am very, very, weak and the good doctor indicates that his regimen for my recovery must, unfortunately, make me feel worse yet before my condition improves.[106] I sense, however, that the end may be near.

I recall Teilhard's confidence to me as early as 1912 that his life was being threatened. I remember he told me that it was the Evangelicals he believed were after his neck. I also remember why.

Damn the Evangelicals and their mediaeval dogma! They must be stopped! They must not be permitted to slow— much less, halt—the progress of mankind. There are some persons who feel that they should simply be killed off to stave the tide of Evangelicalism. But that would be answering lunacy with lunacy. There are others, like myself, who would simply legislate—and enforce!—laws to keep them out of the public business.

---

[105] Pyorrhea alveolaris is an inflammatory condition involving the gingival (gum) tissues and periodontal membrane. It is often associated with a discharge of pus from the alveoli (the tooth sockets) and a loosening of the teeth in their sockets.

[106] Dawson wrote to Smith Woodward on February 6, 1916: "I have been

I yearn to think what the current state of humanity would be were it not for orthodox religion—any organised, orthodox religion. For one thing, we would have had five hundred more years of scientific knowledge were it not for the Roman Church's historical tether on non-Biblical enquiry. *Five hundred years!* The solution to my present illness would be child's play for the medical community. There would have been no wars whose roots could be found in religious differences. Society at large would be that much the wealthier for not having to support, maintain, and protect the lands and possessions of the Church with public monies. The poorer among us would be materially richer for not being required to pay taxes to assist in the preservation of the Church's possessions, right down to paying for fire brigades to extinguish their fires (the Church does not contribute to extinguishing a fire in my home). I am sure that the Church will continue to squeeze every last farthing from an already-suffering population in order to maintain its valuable land-holdings, its massive art collections, and its other private possessions. And the clergy will continue to exact indulgences from their flock in the form of "contributions" and "alms"—not to expunge transgressions, as they did in the past, but to convince their poor, wandering sheep that this "sharing" will help gain them the

---

very ill, and am to have injections of serum in London which will make me worse, temporarily."

grace of God so that they may all enter the Kingdom of Heaven.

Who in the world is as rich as the Roman Church? Has there ever been a sovereign state with such a long history of wealth? Has there ever been a sovereign state with such a long history of global influence?

It must end. The Church must give back what it has taken from its followers over the past two thousand years. Perhaps if it shared its wealth, one fewer waif would die on the streets of London, or one fewer hard-working labourer would have to pay one fewer shilling in taxes to supply sewage services to one fewer cathedral.

This maniacal lunacy must stop. *It must stop!*

And so, at long last, will my death not be the result of natural causes? Am I slowly and deliberately being murdered by an unknown and unseen assassin who is acting "in God's name"?

I could not let on to Dr Fawssett that this might be the case; for if I did, a Pandora's Box would fly open. I would be forced to answer too many questions. *Why did I think I was being assassinated? Who was after me? Why did they want to kill me?* If I allowed these questions to be asked, the hoax would be exposed immediately. I must put faith in my physician's ability to heal me.

My physician! What if it is *my physician* who is acting as a murderous surrogate for the Evangelicals? What if it is *he* who is slowly stifling my life's breath? God, *no!* I must not think like that!

Am I going mad? *Am I going to die a madman?*[107]
Sleep . . . must sleep . . .

When I awoke, Doyle was sitting on a chair beside my
bed. He told me he had just returned from the Front in
France.

"I received your wire, Conan. Thank God Teilhard is
still alive!" I said from my sick-bed.

"Alive and very well, Charles. And I see that you are
also on the mend. What does your physician say about
the prognosis for your recovery?"

I explained my condition to Doyle and told him about
my doctor's admonition about feeling worse before I felt
better. I also confided to Doyle that I feared my doctor
might be my assassin, to which he responded: "There,
there, Charles. I know Fawssett very well. He has an
exemplary reputation. I can assure you that he is doing
all he can to rid you of your infection."

"Thank you for your support, Conan. I appreciate it.
Now, please tell me of your travels to France and what
you know of Teilhard's circumstance."

---

[107] At this point, Dawson may have already been suffering from the delirium
of septicemia, the condition that would eventually kill him. Septicemia is
an invasion of the bloodstream by virulent micro-organisms from a focus of
infection. It is marked by chills, fever and prostration (physical exhaustion),
and often by the formation of secondary abscesses in various organs. Advanced
cases of septicemia can be accompanied by hallucinatory paranoia. The disease
is commonly called "blood poisoning."

"The over-all impression I have of the war is simple",
Doyle began. "I hate war.[108] Be that as it may, Charles,
when I arrived, I was made to wear one of those soup-
plate shrapnel-helmets and, under a fiery sun, I stumbled
and slipped through the clay of communications trenches
to the British front-line. I lunched with General Sir
Douglas Haig . . ."

"Haig? You had lunch with Haig, the Commander-
in-Chief of the British forces?"

"Yes, Charles. But you must remember that my trip
was set up by the Foreign Office. I had nothing whatsoever to do with arranging a meeting with Sir Douglas."

"My word", I said, "General Haig!"

"Yes, Charles", Doyle said again with a smile. "But,
wonderful as it was, that was not the highlight of my
travels. For several days later, I travelled to the French
Front, where I was warmly greeted by a brass band, the
instruments polished to a mirror finish. General Humbert
was the host at a dinner in my honour. And a sumptuous
affair it was at that. Roast beef, freshly-baked bread, a
variety of vegetables, salads, desserts and, of course,
French wine."

"There are advantages to being a high-ranking officer
in the army", I said.

"Oh, yes, that is certain, Charles. Now, Humbert,

---

[108] Indeed he did. Doyle wrote, "May God's curse rest upon the arrogant
men and the unholy ambitions which let loose this horror upon humanity!"

it turns out, is an avid follower of my *Sherlock Holmes* adventures. At one point he asked me: 'Sherlock Holmes, *est-ce qu'il est un soldat dans l'armée anglaise?*' I did not know how to respond, so I simply said: '*Mais, mon général, il est trop vieux pour service!*'

"I felt quite comfortable with General Humbert and, fortunately, he with me, so while we were having one last glass of wine after dinner I said, 'General, if I may, I should like to ask a favour of you.'

" 'Certainly, Dr Doyle', he said, 'what is it I can do for you?'

" 'Sir, I am trying to find a friend of mine. His name is Marie-Joseph Pierre Teilhard de Chardin. He is a Catholic priest serving as a *bancardier* with the Fourth Combined Tirailleurs and Zouaves. I fear his life is in jeopardy at the hand of an assassin. Please spare me the need for giving the reason, but I should appreciate it very much if you could find him and direct me to him.'

" 'I will do all I can to help you, Dr Doyle. I will contact the Fourth by wireless tonight and have the infor mation you request in the morning.' "

"So", I said with a smile, interrupting Doyle's narrative, "you managed to secure the assistance of the French Army in our adventure!"

"Yes, Charles, and with striking results, as you will soon learn.

"I breakfasted with the General's chief aide the next morning", Doyle continued. "He told me that the

General had already managed to find Teilhard, and that I was to be escorted to him by several soldiers after our meal. Needless to say, Charles, I finished my breakfast quickly. It was at this point, when I learnt that Teilhard was still alive, that I wired my message to you.

"The aide handed me a letter of introduction signed by General Humbert requesting that I be given every assistance. This letter would prove to be a very powerful document indeed.

"I was given the uniform of a French infantryman, and wore the medical insignia. It quite reminded me of my experience as a youth in the Boer War. After half a day's journey in a military vehicle which took us through the Argonne Forest and on to Verdun, we stopped for a late lunch. Sitting in the relative calm of a service tent, I could hear the incessant rattle of small-arms fire and the explosion of cannon. This experience was quite different from the peaceful conditions under which you first introduced me to Teilhard at the restaurant in Crowborough. The memory of that meeting strengthened my resolve to see him and warn him of the danger he was in.

"After lunch, we climbed back into the vehicle and drove in the direction of the headquarters for the Fourth. We finally arrived there about five o'clock in the afternoon.

"I was taken to the hospital area. One of my escorts pointed to a small tent tucked in the woods and said,

'*Voilà!*' I paced briskly towards the tent, pulled back the flap at the entrance, and went in. It was empty, save for a solitary soul sitting at a table and writing by the light of a kerosene lamp.

" '*Excusez-moi, s'il vous plaît,*' I said, '*peut-être vous êtes Père Pierre Teilhard de Chardin?*'

"Teilhard turned in his seat—out of curiosity, I am sure, because he heard someone speaking French with a British accent—and saw an ageing, weighty soldier in a French cavalryman's uniform that was too tight. He stood, but did not immediately recognise me due to the dim lighting. As he walked towards me, I saw immediately that he had changed."

"Changed? How so, Conan?" I asked.

"Charles, Teilhard wears a moustache!"

"A moustache? I cannot believe it. I cannot imagine what he would look like wearing a moustache."

With those words, Doyle reached into his coat pocket and withdrew a photograph of Teilhard, proudly sporting his French Army uniform and an elegant moustache.

"Ha!" I barked.

" '*Conan! Conan!*' " Doyle continued his story. " '*What a wonderful surprise. I can barely believe it is you!*' he said, as we embraced, shook hands, and embraced yet again.

" '*Pierre*', I said, 'warmest greetings from Charles, Hélène and Jean.'

Father Pierre Teilhard de Chardin

" 'Conan, please excuse my tears of joy. More than anything else, more than *anything*, I miss my friends, and you and Charles most of all.'

"Then we sat down and brought each other up to date. The conversation soon turned to the Piltdown affair and, more specifically, to our fear that Teilhard would be assassinated."

" 'How did you hear about that, Conan?' he asked.

" 'Hear about what?' I asked in response.

" 'About the attempt on my life.'

" 'Somebody tried to kill you?'

" 'Yes, about a week ago.'

" 'That is precisely why I came to see you. I came to warn you of an assassination attempt.'

" *'But how did you know somebody was going to try to kill me?'*

"At that point, Charles, I told Teilhard about the murders in Ilford and at Barkham Manor, and about the Sussex Evangelical Association. After my summary, all he could do was hold his hand to his head and say, *'Mon Dieu!'*

" 'Pierre', I said, 'I think we should be able to find the person who attempted to murder you. He must still be among the soldiers here, for there is no other place for him to go. I will request a general roll-call for to-morrow morning, at which time I am certain we shall be able to identify the assassin.'

" 'By what authority can you request a general roll-call?' Teilhard asked.

" 'By *this* authority', I said, and I handed him the letter from General Humbert.

" *'Mon Dieu!'* "

"The following morning, a bugle summoned the whole of the Fourth Combined Tirailleurs and Zouaves to roll-call. Teilhard and I were escorted by two officers as we walked past the soldiers one by one. After requesting that they remove their head-gear, I looked every one of them in the eye. Ten, twenty, fifty, then a hundred and fifty. We walked through rows and rows of soldiers. And then I stopped at a single infantryman.

" 'Preston!' I shouted. *'Jonathan Preston, step forward!'*

" 'My name is not Preston, sir', he said. 'It is Smith.'

" 'Your name is Jonathan Preston! You attempted last week to assassinate the man standing next to me! *Now step forward!'*

"Realising that I meant business, he bolted from the group and into the woods.

"Teilhard, the two officers accompanying us, and I tore after him. The officers caught him and held him still as Teilhard and I looked at him. 'This, Pierre, is your would-be assassin', I said. 'He is a member of the Sussex Evangelical Association. He was engaged by that organisation to find and murder you. He was able to gain access to membership in the Fourth, I am sure, through the influence of his leader, one Barton Thackery. I am now convinced that the tentacles of the Evangelicals must also reach into the higher echelons of the military, for I can think of no other method for a non-military British subject to become a soldier in a French detachment.'

"I asked that the officers confine Preston under the charge of attempted murder, upon which Preston was disarmed, handcuffed, and led off to gaol. He will be court-martialled under military law, convicted, I am sure, and most likely will spend the rest of his life in prison.

Interestingly, Charles, as Preston was led away, he turned to Teilhard and sneered '*Heretic!*' at him."

"Thank God Teilhard is safe, Conan", I said with a sigh of relief. "If Teilhard does survive the remainder of the War, there is no telling what contributions he can make to science and philosophy. He is indeed a unique individual."

"That he is, Charles. That he is."

"So, Conan", I asked expectantly, "can we at long last close this case?"

"Not quite yet", said Doyle. "There is one more loose end."

"Which is . . . ?"

"Thackery."

"*Thackery*", I thought to myself after Doyle had left. "*That scoundrel Thackery. I hope that murderer gets his just desserts. And if anyone can serve them up to him, it is Doyle. Oh, I wish I were a healthy man. My God, how I wish I had my health!*"

A week later, Doyle visited me to bring me up to date on his activities. He told me then that he had gone to Ilford and found that the Sussex Evangelical Association's headquarters had been abandoned. Nothing remained in the building save a small table, four chairs and an empty bookcase. Doyle did, however, enter the back room and found the remnants of a printing operation. Apparently, the Evangelicals had used it for preparing their propaganda.

"I visited the Sussex County Clerk's Office to see if they had any information on his whereabouts", Doyle told me. "They had only the Ilford address on record. Apparently, Thackery also used the place as a residence. I then went to London and visited my acquaintance at the Foreign Office. I asked him if there was any way I could determine if Thackery were still in the country and, if so, how I might find him."

"And were you able to?" I asked.

"No, because he is no longer in England."

"Where on earth is he, then?"

"He is in America."

"America?" I blurted out. "What is he doing in America?"

"He filed for and received emigration papers about three weeks ago", Doyle said, "at about the time Preston attempted to murder Teilhard. The application he filed indicated that his ultimate destination was Macon County in the state of Tennessee. It is clear that Thackery had no plans for waiting to hear from Preston about the success or failure of the mission. He may even have left for the States on the very day of the assassination attempt."

"So Thackery is gone, slipped out of the country", I said with some disappointment.

"Yes, Charles, he is gone. My guess is that he will try

to contact one of the Evangelical groups in the United States. He will no doubt disappear into the scenery."

"*Macon County, Tennessee?*" I asked myself. "*Why, of all places in the world, Macon County, Tennessee?*"

And now, dear Reader, I promised at the beginning of this narrative "incontestable and undeniable" proof that it was I who perpetrated the Piltdown hoax. This is the easiest chore of all, for I had the presence of mind to retain the mandibular symphysis and the condylar fragment severed from the doctored orang-utan jaw. I entrusted them to Doyle for safe-keeping. It will be learnt some day, of course, that these fragments fit perfectly with the mandible now being held in the British Museum's collection.

Upon my death, which I fear is imminent, Arthur Conan Doyle and Doyle alone will know the precise site of the only existing physical proof of my role in the Piltdown hoax.

I can only pray that he will use this knowledge wisely.

Finis

ANNOTATOR'S AFTERWORD

In 1921, my grandfather met a Macon County, Tennessee, farmer named John Washington Butler. Butler was a devout man who attended church every Sunday, and my relative, an itinerant preacher who had emigrated to the United States in 1916, would often lead the church services. During one of his sermons, he mentioned that a young woman in the community had gone away to be educated at a university. Not only had she returned home with a Bachelor of Arts degree, but she also returned believing in the theory of evolution and not believing in the existence of God. "What might happen to your children?" my grandfather asked his congregation. "No need even to go to the university to be corrupted. Darwin's theory of evolution is taught right here in the public high schools of Macon County." This story set Butler to thinking of his own children. What might happen to them?

Butler ran for and won a seat on the state legislature the next year. He was renominated for office in 1924, having run with the promise that, if re-elected, he would do something about the lie of evolution being taught in the public schools. He won his seat again, and introduced the following bill, known as the Butler Act.

AN ACT prohibiting the teaching of the Evolution Theory in all the Universities, Normals, and all other public schools of Tennessee, which are supported in whole or in part by the public school funds of the State, and to provide penalties for the violations thereof.

Section 1. Be it enacted by the General Assembly of the State of Tennessee, That it shall be unlawful for any teacher in any of the Universities, Normals and all other public schools of the State which are supported in whole or in part by the public school funds of the State, to teach any theory that denies the story of the Divine Creation of man as taught in the Bible, and to teach instead that man has descended from a lower order of animals.

Section 2. Be it further enacted, That any teacher found guilty of the violation of this Act shall be guilty of a misdemeanor and, upon conviction, shall be fined not less than One Hundred Dollars ($100.00) nor more than Five Hundred Dollars ($500.00) for each offense.

Section 3. Be it further enacted, That this Act take effect from and after its passage, the public welfare requiring it.

As the world now knows, John Thomas Scopes, a Dayton High School biology teacher, was accused of violating the Butler Act, and was brought to trial in 1925. Thus, my grandfather was, in part, responsible for Scopes's trial, and instrumental in his conviction and hundred-dollar fine.

Given this background, I should not have been so surprised at having discovered an even darker episode in his life.

I first began to understand how truly unsavory a man my ancestor was while examining documents on file in the Macon County Clerk's Office. The records, which included his residence papers, led to a trip to England, to a town called Ilford. My further investigations there finally guided me to the papers of a certain Mr. Lewis Abbott, in which I found the incriminating evidence against my grandfather, linking him to theft and at least two unsolved murders. I thereby resolved to do two things:

My first objective was to dissociate myself completely from my detestable Evangelist relative by means of a change of name.

Exposing his treachery was my second objective. The story about him is true. But Charles Dawson's memoir about the Piltdown hoax is itself a fraud. *I* wrote it.

Charles Conan

ACKNOWLEDGMENTS

I would like, first of all, to thank three close friends for reading, commenting on, and undoubtedly influencing the improvement of the manuscript: Dan Barnhart, a twentieth-century Renaissance Man, who followed this project from its inception, syllable by syllable; Warren Rowlinson, a formidable three-cushion billiards opponent, who made many valuable suggestions; and Paul Mazzacano, who read a very early draft of the manuscript and unfortunately did not live to see the final version.

I am grateful to the staff of the Santa Clara (California) Public Library (Main Branch) for their untiring assistance with this project. And to John Thackray, archivist for the Royal Geological Society of London, and Ms. Angharad Hills, Staff Editor and Secretary to the Publications Committee at the Royal Geological Society Publishing House, both of whom supplied photographs.

To Peggy Walsh of *The New York Times*, I offer my appreciation for assistance with permitting the reproduction of articles that are now more than eighty years old. Appreciation must also go to Elaine Hart of the Picture Library at *The Illustrated London News* and to Penny Eckley of Oxford University Press (London) for their kind assistance. And for the valuable help given to me by Lodvina Mascarenhas, Permissions Officer at the British Museum (Natural History), to simplify the time-consuming process of obtaining photographs.

Dr. W. W. Howells, a trailblazer in the field of modern paleoanthropology, gave his kind permission to reproduce illustrations from his book, *Mankind So Far* (Garden City, NY: Doubleday & Co., 1946).

I would also like to thank Mary A. Read of Prometheus Books of Buffalo, New York, for her help, as well as Peggy Conversano at the American Museum of Natural History's *Natural History* magazine.

An extra dose of appreciation must go to the genuine students of the Piltdown affair: Frank Spencer (*Piltdown: A Scientific Forgery* and *The Piltdown Papers*); Charles Blinderman (*The Piltdown Inquest*); Ronald Millar (*The Piltdown Men*); and J. S. Weiner (*The Piltdown Forgery*). Without those scholars, this book could not have been written. It is they who are the *real* Piltdown men.

Finally, I would like to thank Robert Wyatt, president of A Wyatt Book for St. Martin's Press, for his invaluable support, encouragement, and liberal use of advice and experience. Special thanks to Mr. Wyatt's assistant, Iris Bass, whose early and unwavering faith in this project helped guide it gently from dream to reality.

ENDNOTES

PAGE vii: "Paleolithic Skull Is a Missing Link," courtesy of The New York Times Company. Reprinted by permission.

PAGE ix: *Photograph of Charles Dawson courtesy of the Geological Society of London.*

PAGE 1: *impugn my credentials for intellectual honesty*
This is not the only time Dawson had a shadow of dishonesty cast over him. J. S. Weiner points out in his classic *The Piltdown Forgery* (London, 1955) that although Dawson's two-volume history of Hastings Castle had achieved wide circulation, "it was early recognized as less a product of genuine scholarship than of extensive plagiarism" (p. 176).

PAGE 4: *where we would often muse over "Ice-Age Man"*
Stephen Jay Gould, in *The Panda's Thumb* (New York: W. W. Norton & Co., 1982), recognizes the fraternity between Dawson and Teilhard: "I can easily imagine Dawson and Teilhard, over long hours in field and pub, hatching a plot for different reasons: Dawson to expose the gullibility of pompous professionals; Teilhard to rub English noses once again with the taunt that their nation [as opposed to France] had no legitimate human fossils. . . ." (p. 114).

PAGES 6–7: Both illustrations courtesy of W. W. Howells, *Mankind So Far* (Garden City, NY: Doubleday & Co., 1946).

PAGE 9: *I met my first co-conspirator*
The two men met quite by accident, it seems, in a stone quarry outside of
Hastings, on May 31, 1909. It is the first indication of any visit to Piltdown
by Teilhard. Mary and Ellen Lukas tell the story in *Teilhard: The Man, the
Priest, the Scientist* (New York: Doubleday & Co., 1977): "Teilhard and a
Jesuit friend, Félix Pelletier, were poking around about a gravel pit near the
theologate, where they found another dig in progress. Suddenly, up popped
a round-faced, bouncy man in a straw hat, vest, and shirt sleeves, wielding
a trowel. Spectacles glinting and ruddy face aglow, he rushed to pump the
visitors' hands. 'You're geologists!' he exclaimed."

PAGE 9: *in Egypt for a three-year stay*
Teilhard taught physics and chemistry in Ismalia, Egypt, from 1905 to
1908. It was this period, according to Joseph V. Kopp, that "was to have
lasting influence on [Teilhard's] love for the earth. It was here that he first
realized the meaning of evolution, that the whole world is in a continuous,
irresistible state of becoming, rising from a previous 'Less' to an even more
refined 'More.' "

PAGE 10: *bemoan the Roman Church's intractably dogmatic theology*
Later in 1918, while reading a book written by Edouard Schuré, "a mind
extremely sympathetic to my own," Teilhard wrote in a letter to his cousin,
Marguerite Teillard-Chambon, ". . . I feel my conviction of the necessity
for the Church to present dogma in a more real, more universal, way—a
more 'cosmogenic' way, if I may put it so. Human consciousness and the
very nature of dogma demand this." From *Pierre Teilhard de Chardin: The
Making of a Mind—Letters from a Soldier-Priest*, translated by René Hague
(New York: Harper & Row, 1961), pp. 267–268.

PAGE 12: *Barkham Manor in Piltdown*
Charles Blinderman opens his book with the following etymology of "Piltdown": "After the Saxons had settled down [1300 years ago in what was
originally called Suth Seaxna], a fellow named Pileca took possession of the
hill, or dun, and Pileca's dun developed into Pylkedoune, whence
Peltedowne in the seventeenth century." *The Piltdown Inquest* (Buffalo, NY:
Prometheus Books, 1986), p. 3.

PAGE 12: *Footnote 15*
Spencer points out that "This familiar entourage, armed with picks and
shovels, set tongues wagging, and had mobilized the local constabulary, as
Woodward recalled" [in *The Earliest Englishman*, London, 1948]. Frank
Spencer, *Piltdown: A Scientific Forgery* (London and New York: Oxford Univer-
sity Press, 1990), p. 160.

PAGE 14: Photograph courtesy of the Natural History Museum, London.

PAGE 28: *Millenarianistic movement that emerged during this century*
Millenarianism (also called Millenialism) was a belief held in the early Church which proclaimed that the saints would rule the earth for a thousand years before the Second Coming of Christ. This belief was revived by the Anabaptists during the Reformation and, more recently, by the Adventists. Its basis is found in Revelation 20:1–7

1 And I saw an angel come down from heaven, having the key of the bottomless pit and a great chain in his hand.

2 And he laid hold on the dragon, that old serpent, which is the Devil, and Satan, and bound him a thousand years,

3 And cast him into the bottomless pit, and shut him up, and set a seal upon him, that he should deceive the nations no more, till the thousand years should be fulfilled; and after that he must be loosed a little season [i.e., for a little while].

4 And I saw thrones, and they sat upon them, and judgment was given unto them: and I saw the souls of them that were beheaded for the witness of Jesus, and for the word of God, and which had not worshipped the beast, neither his image, neither had received his mark upon their foreheads, or in their hands; and they lived and reigned with Christ a thousand years.

5 But the rest of the dead lived not again until the thousand years were finished. This is the first resurrection.

6 Blessed and holy is he that hath part in the first resurrection: on such the second death hath no power, but they shall be priests of God and of Christ, and shall reign with him a thousand years.

7 And when the thousand years are expired, Satan shall be loosed out of his prison.

PAGE 28: *bedlam brought about by Modernism*
Henry M. Morris, biblical literalist *extraordinaire* and president of the Institute for Creation Research, tells us what the fundamentalist position is in regard to Modernism: "Religious liberalism (or 'modernism,' as it was also called) continued to dominate institutionalized Christianity throughout most of the first half of the twentieth century, and it was based squarely on evolutionism. It not only accepted naturalistic evolution instead of supernatural creation in science and history, but it also embraced the idea that evolution had produced religion itself. Their 'higher criticism' of the Bible was based on this completely invalid notion." (*The Long War Against God* [Grand Rapids, MI: Baker Book House Co., 1989], p. 97). Morris goes on to say: "If the written Word was considered to be the product of evolution, so was the living Word. Jesus Christ was no longer accepted as the unique Son of God but simply as a highly evolved human being, perhaps the pinnacle

of the evolutionary process. His resurrection became a 'spiritual' resurrection and the virgin birth was rejected altogether. His miracles were explained naturalistically, and his death on the cross was like that of any other martyr, with no particular saving efficacy except as an example" (p. 98). Teilhard did in fact believe that Jesus Christ was "the pinnacle of the evolutionary process." This "heresy" put him at odds with the Roman Catholic Church.

PAGE 29: *God's revelation of Himself to Man*
After Henry A. Virkler, *Hermeneutics: Principles and Processes of Biblical Interpretation* (Grand Rapids, MI: Baker Book House Co., 1981). According to Richard Elliott Friedman, "The term 'Higher Criticism' was used to distinguish [historical inquiry] from textual studies, which was referred to as 'Lower Criticism.' In textual study, a biblical scholar compares the various oldest surviving manuscripts of the Bible—the Masoretic Hebrew text, the Greek versions, the Vulgate (Latin), the Aramaic, and now the Qumran ('Dead Sea Scrolls') texts, among others. When the versions differ, the scholar tries to determine which is the original and which is the result of a scribal error or emendation. Often fascinating and important for biblical interpretation, this study of the words of the text itself was nevertheless regarded as 'lower' (though not necessarily in a negative sense) than the study of content and history involved in the study of the sources." *Who Wrote the Bible?* (New York: Summit Books, 1987), p. 262, note 4.

PAGE 29: *Hegel*
Georg Wilhelm Friedrich Hegel (1770–1831), the German philosopher, maintained that dialectical law governs the process of reality: every thesis implies its own contradiction or antitheses (as Will Durant put it in *The Story of Philosophy* (New York: Simon and Schuster, 1926, 1961, p. 223) "an open mind and a cautious hand, an open hand and a cautious mind . . ."). "The task of religion [according to Hegel] is to reach and feel that Absolute in which all opposites are resolved into unity, that great sum of being in which matter and mind, subject and object, good and evil, are one." (Durant, p. 224). The source of the struggle Teilhard had with Hegelian-like unification of the seemingly antithetical concepts of Christianity and evolution now becomes clear.

PAGE 30: *my old friend*
Dawson and Doyle had known each other for years. Doyle had an active interest in anthropology and archeology. By the time of this dinner meeting (1912) Doyle had published his first attempt at science fiction, a book entitled *The Lost World*. Julian Symons describes the story in *Conan Doyle: Portrait of an Artist* (New York: The Mysterious Press, 1979): "[*The Lost World*] . . . the first, and much the best, of these [science fiction] novels is about a journey to Amazonia, where Professor Challenger claims to have

traced some prehistoric animals still living on a great plateau. The irascible Challenger, a figure based on the professor of anatomy at Edinburgh [where Doyle attended medical school], takes a party of adventurous spirits to look for the lost world. Their adventures are marked by that speculative ingenuity which was one of Conan Doyle's most engaging marks as man and writer, and by an imaginative quality that came into play most fully when he was dealing with scenes outside everyday life. The description of the Amazonian forest obviously owes something to the author's travels, yet it has a kind of spectral quality that removes it from literal reality" (pp. 94 and 98).

PAGE 31: *Still looking for "Ice-Age Man?"*
Doyle has been accused of complicity in the Piltdown hoax before. John Hathaway Winslow and Alfred Meyer describe in a magazine article the "labyrinthine trail" that led them to believe that Doyle may very well have been in on the fraud from the beginning ("The Perpetrator at Piltdown," *Science 83* [September 1983], pp. 83–98). Winslow and Meyer present what they admit is (very strong) circumstantial evidence, with great emphasis on Doyle's personal travels and his story *The Lost World.*

PAGE 32: *a dozen bishoprics in England*
After Symons, *Conan Doyle: Portrait of an Artist.*

PAGE 33: *like a summons unanswered*
After Pierre Teilhard de Chardin, *The Heart of the Matter* (New York: Harcourt Brace Jovanovich, 1978), p. 25.

PAGE 34: *a curve that all lines must follow*
Pierre Teilhard de Chardin, *The Phenomenon of Man* (New York: Harper & Row, 1965), p. 219.

PAGE 34: *God cannot create, except evolutively*
Pierre Teilhard de Chardin, *Christianity and Evolution* (New York: Harcourt Brace Jovanovich, 1971), p. 179.

PAGE 34: *immune from any subsequent contradiction by experience*
Chardin, *The Phenomenon of Man,* p. 140.

PAGE 35: *Pauline doctrine of Christ recapitulating everything in Himself*
After a letter from Teilhard to A. Vandel.

PAGE 35: *a parallelism between complexity and consciousness*
After Bernard Delfgaauw, *Evolution: The Theory of Teilhard de Chardin,* translated by Hubert Hoskins (New York: Harper & Row, 1969), pp. 29–30.

PAGE 36: *to support faith by actual provable fact*
Written by Doyle for a chapter called "The Psychic Question As I See It"
for Carl Murchison, ed., *The Case For and Against Psychic Belief* (Worcester,
MA, 1927), p. 15, quoted in Trevor H. Hall, *Sherlock Holmes and His Creator*
(New York: St. Martin's Press, 1977), p. 95. Hall continues the quote in
which Doyle gives a brief history of his dealings with psychic research.
Doyle's words indicate how completely captured he was by the spiritualist
movement: "I would first state my credentials, since my opinion is only of
value in so far as these are valid. In 1886, being at that time a materialist,
I was induced to examine psychic phenomena. In 1887 I wrote a signed
article in *Light* upon the question. From that time I have never ceased to
keep in touch with the matter by reading and occasional experiment. My
conversion to the full meaning of spiritualism was a very gradual one, but
by the war time it was complete. In 1916 I gave a lecture upon the subject,
and found that it gave strength and comfort to others. I therefore determined
to devote all my time to it, and so in the last ten years I have concentrated on
it, testing very many mediums, good and bad, studying extensive literature,
keeping in close touch with current psychic research, and incidentally writing
seven books on the subject. It is not possible that any living man can have
had a much larger experience. When I add that I am a Doctor of medicine,
specially trained in observation, and that as a public man of affairs I have
never shown myself to be wild or unreasonable, I hope I have persuaded you
that my opinion should have some weight as compared to those opponents
whose contempt for the subject has been so great that it has prevented them
from giving calm consideration to the facts" (p. 95).

PAGE 41: *reject the true Word of God*
After Jimmy Swaggart, *Catholicism and Christianity* (Baton Rouge, LA:
Jimmy Swaggart Ministries, 1986), pp. 10–11.

PAGE 42: *customary in the Church for a long time*
After Albert J. Nevins, *Answering a Fundamentalist* (Huntington, IN: Our
Visitor Publishing Company, 1990), pp. 25ff.

PAGE 42: *Stand up: I myself also am a man*
Swaggart, *Catholicism and Christianity*, p. 12. Swaggart describes Peter as
being "claimed by the Catholic hierarchy as the prototype for all popes."

PAGE 43: *the "substantial authenticity" . . . must be taught*
After Ian G. Balbour, *Issues in Science and Religion* (New York: Harper & Row
1966), p. 100. Fathers Leroy and Zahn were early Catholic supporters of
both evolution and higher criticism. They encountered disapproval from the
Church, and their ideas were never widely circulated.

PAGE 45: *something essentially different appeared on the scene*
After Delfgaauw, *Evolution: The Theory of Teilhard de Chardin*, p. 28.

PAGE 47: *development of the brain*
Adapted from ibid.

PAGE 50: *agreed to dwell apart as long as Louise lived*
After Don Richard Cox, *Arthur Conan Doyle* (New York: Frederick Ungar Publishing Co., 1985), p. 6.

PAGE 50: *Jean has soft brown hair*
The description of Jean Leckie is adapted from Charles Higham's *The Adventures of Conan Doyle* (New York: W.W. Norton & Co., 1976), p. 148.

PAGE 60: Illustration courtesy of the Geological Society of London.

PAGE 61: Illustration reproduced from Grafton Elliot Smith, *The Evolution of Man* (London: Oxford University Press, 1924).

PAGE 65: Illustration at top in text courtesy of the Geological Society of London.

PAGE 65: *Footnote 55.* Illustration by Mark Mancevice, "Critical Mistake" from Charles Blinderman, *The Piltdown Inquest* (Buffalo, N.Y.: Prometheus Books). Copyright © 1986 by Charles Blinderman. Reprinted by permission of the publisher.

PAGES 77–78: *Arthur Smith Woodward, my precise contemporary*
Biographical data for Smith Woodward is based on information contained in Frank Spencer's two books, *Piltdown: A Scientific Forgery* and *The Piltdown Papers*, both published by Oxford University Press (London and New York, 1990). Illustration courtesy of the Geological Society of London.

PAGE 80: Map by Henry Fairfield Osborn, courtesy of *Natural History* magazine, The American Museum of Natural History.

PAGE 85: *Footnote 64:* "Pleistocene Skull Found in England," courtesy of The New York Times Company. Reprinted by permission.

PAGE 85: *Examples of the correspondence follow*
The source for the correspondence is Frank Spencer's *The Piltdown Papers*.

PAGE 90: *without any error*
Adapted from A. A. Hodge and Benjamin B. Wardield, "Inspiration," *The Presbyterian Review* 2 (April 1881).

PAGE 93: *depart from the dogmatic prescription*
After Lloyd J. Averill, *Religious Right, Religious Wrong: A Critique of the Fundamentalist Phenomenon*, (New York: The Pilgrim Press, 1989), p. 9.

PAGE 100: *Footnote 79:* "Man Had Reason Before He Spoke," courtesy of The New York Times Company. Reprinted by permission.

PAGES 105–108: Photographs courtesy of *The Illustrated London News*.

PAGE 112: Illustration courtesy of the Geological Society of London.

PAGE 113: *evidence that could vindicate his reconstruction of the Piltdown skull*
Much later, Smith Woodward wrote in *The Earliest Englishman*: "We were then excavating a rather deep and hot trench in which Father Teilhard, in black clothing, was especially energetic; and, as we thought he seemed a little exhausted, we suggested that he should leave us to do the hard labour for a time while he had comparative rest in searching the rain-washed spread gravel. Very soon he exclaimed that he had picked up the missing canine tooth, but we were incredulous, and told him we had already seen several bits of ironstone, which looked like teeth, on the spot where he stood. He insisted, however, that he was not deceived, so we both left our digging to go and verify his discovery. There could be no doubt about it, and we all spent the rest of the day until dusk crawling over the gravel in the vain quest for more." Quoted in Spencer, *Piltdown: A Scientific Forgery*, p. 69.

PAGE 115: *neither budging so much as an intellectual inch*
Keith later wrote in his *Autobiography* (London: 1950), "I shall never forget the angry look [Smith Woodward] gave me [as they walked out of the meeting]. Such was the end of a long friendship."

PAGE 116: *Foonote 85*
Ronald Millar comments in *The Piltdown Men* (New York: St. Martin's Press, 1972) that "This sensational feat was the talk of scientific circles for many a day" (p. 138).

PAGE 117: *what once served as an oast-house*
Spencer describes the Barkham property thus: "[The] Victorian Manor House has a large hall, four reception rooms, six bedrooms, and three bathrooms, and stands on 35 acres of land. Directly associated are several other buildings, a four-bedroomed oast-house (standing on the west side of the drive and

looking directly down on the gravel bed site) and a thatched barn." *Piltdown: A Scientific Forgery*, p. 232, note 3.

PAGE 117: *Footnote 86*
Mabel Kenward lived until 1978.

PAGE 125: *him will my Father honour. Amen*
Adapted from Swaggart, *Catholicism and Christianity*, pp. 216–217.

PAGE 126: *go to Hell in the end!*
Sunday's sermon is a conflation of his actual words and peripheral commentary of Roger A. Bruns from Bruns' book, *Preacher: Billy Sunday and Big-Time American Evangelism* (New York: W.W. Norton & Co., 1992).

PAGE 149: *a ferocious moustache*
Blinderman, *The Piltdown Inquest*, p. 194.

PAGE 151: *at least one branch of modern man*
Adapted from Blinderman, pp. 203–204.

PAGE 151: Illustration courtesy of the Geological Society of London.

PAGE 153: *Abbott's own private collection*
After Blinderman, *The Piltdown Inquest*, p. 204.

PAGE 155: *No one was hurt*
After Robert Speaight, *Teilhard de Chardin: A Biography* (London: Collins, 1967), p. 61.

PAGE 156: *I must know*
Teilhard de Chardin, *The Heart of the Matter*, pp. 168–170.

PAGE 157: *not worth the mud of Douaumont*
Ibid., p. 178.

PAGE 157: *"you're the Piltdown man."*
Ibid., p. 59.

PAGE 157: *during these tumultuous times*
Don Richard Cox, in his biography, *Arthur Conan Doyle*, writes about the fervent interest Doyle had in following the Great War: "Conan Doyle's work on World War I is his six-volume work *The British Campaign in France and Flanders* (1916–1920), his longest single project. The first volume appeared in November, 1916, and the series advanced at a rapid rate, with Doyle

completing five more volumes in just over three years. Although the first volume sold very well, going through three printings in two months, each succeeding volume drew less attention and sales fell off proportionately." Cox also points out Doyle's prescience by describing a 1914 short story called "Danger!'": "In this piece of fiction Doyle envisioned what would happen if a fleet of enemy submarines surrounded Great Britain and cut off all shipping. The startling efficiency of this fictional attack that forces Britain to surrender in a matter of weeks was proof, Doyle felt, of the island's basic vulnerability to German U-boats. His foresight was unfortunately proved to be valid a few years later during World War I when German submarines were able to strike with all the precision Doyle had predicted" (p. 11).

PAGE 158: Illustration courtesy of the Geological Society of London.

PAGE 164: *known as the Dengie Hundred*
Abbot's biographical information is adapted from J. S. Weiner, *The Piltdown Forgery*.

PAGE 164: *so I made up my mind to learn*
After Blinderman, *The Piltdown Inquest*, p. 194.

PAGE 167: The *Omphalos* story is gleaned from Stephen Jay Gould, *The Flamingo's Smile* (New York: W.W. Norton & Co., 1985).

PAGE 186: *through the clay of communications trenches to the British front-line*
Adapted from John Dickson Carr, *The Life of Sir Arthur Conan Doyle* (New York: Carroll & Graf, 1949), p. 256.

PAGE 187: *"il est trop vieux pour service!"*
Ibid., p. 258.

PAGE 196: *Annotator's Afterword:*
Information and quotations for annotator's grandfather's involvement in the Scopes "Monkey Trial" was adapted from Ray Ginger, *Six Days or Forever: Tennessee v. John Thomas Scopes* (London and New York: Oxford University Press, 1958).